ODD MAN OUT

VINCE LAWSON

Outskirts Press, Inc.
Denver, Colorado

Outskirts Press
http://www.outskirtspress.com

ISBN-10: 1-59800-457-3
ISBN-13: 978-1-59800-457-1

CHAPTER 1

W rigley Field sat dark and quiet in the cold fall air as Dean Davenport stepped off the northbound Red Line train that had taken him from his office in Chicago's Loop and deposited him in the heart of the upscale, north side neighborhood of Wrigleyville. Walking quickly, he set out going east on Addison towards Broadway, with its gay, rainbow colored pylons marking the city's Boystown area.

When he had first moved to Chicago, Boystown had been the center of gay life in the city. Growing up in a small southern town, he never dreamed that he would find a place in which he could feel so comfortable. The neighborhood had been his home for over a decade and he couldn't imagine leaving it. Over the years, as gentrification brought in more straight people and more families, some of the gay population had moved further north to Andersonville. Most of his friends had even moved on, in search of cheaper homes and quieter streets, but so far, he had resisted the pull of the crowd.

It was after seven on a Thursday evening, and he knew he should still be at work. He had a dozen projects that he was behind on and there weren't enough hours in the day to finish everything. Today, however, was his birthday and tonight's dinner was a command performance.

As he approached Portino's restaurant, he felt the same mixture of happiness and melancholy that he had been feeling a lot recently, especially when he was with his friends. He loved them all dearly, but for the past few months something just didn't feel right when they were all together. Part of the problem, he knew, was that he still felt slightly disconnected from everyone. After eight years as a road warrior consultant for a large financial services firm, he had finally given up a life of constant travel to try and find a life with a bit more meaning. But after he stopped traveling week-in and week-out and began spending more time with his friends, he realized that the time that he had spent away had taken a toll.

Glancing at his watch, and seeing how late he was, he started jogging towards the restaurant. He hated being late, but his new job as C.O.O. of one of the country's largest non-profit research organizations was consuming all of his time. In the six months that he had been working there, the only thing he felt that he had actually accomplished was pointing out one thing after another that was wrong with the place. His work weeks were already running upwards of sixty hours and he was beginning to wonder when he would find the time to start making a difference.

He had wanted to leave work early so he could go home and get ready for his birthday dinner. He knew that he would need some time to gear up for the party because he hated celebrating his birthday. His friends knew this and therefore insisted on making a big deal of the event, just for the sheer joy of torturing him. But on his way out of the office, his boss had stopped him and asked him a seemingly innocuous question regarding the financial status of one of their largest grants. That simple question turned into a two hour discussion and they still didn't solve anything.

Because of the delay and his rush to get to the restaurant,

which was made even more difficult by his huge briefcase which was loaded with work that he would still need to do at some point during the evening, he felt the sweat building on his forehead as he bolted through the door.

He had barely taken three steps inside the restaurant when a cheer went up from the bar. Looking over, he saw his friends waving their drinks and calling his name. They were not a shy group. Squeezing his way past the line of people waiting to be seated, he reached the bar and accepted a kiss, a hug and very large martini from Moose Jackson, his best friend in the city. Moose was a bear of a man, in every sense of the word. At six feet five inches and two-hundred and sixty pounds – depending upon how much beer he had consumed - he cut an extremely imposing figure. His dark beard and almost coal-black eyes only added to the image of a giant that you did not want to mess with. As he tried to disentangle himself from the massive bear, Moose grabbed the back of Dean's head and licked him from chin to forehead and back down again.

"What the hell was that for?" Dean asked, as he grabbed a napkin to wipe off his face.

Moose took another swig from his beer before responding. "Lonny called me this afternoon and said that since he couldn't be here to celebrate with us, I should give you a very special hello from him."

"I'll be sure to thank the little prick when I talk to him tomorrow," Dean grumbled, while wondering how one man could produce so much saliva.

"Now, now! Such language!" Moose's partner of ten years, Peter Donnelson, said, as he reached over and wrapped Dean in a bear hug of his own. Peter could have been Moose's brother, they were so similar. Two big men with even bigger hearts. They were the happiest couple he had ever known. As he let go of Dean, Peter wiped some of his husband's residual tongue bath off of his face.

"I know it seems disgusting, but believe me, it comes in handy sometimes," Peter said, with an exaggerated wink.

Everyone laughed, including a somewhat embarrassed straight couple sitting next to Moose, as Dean made his way to the dual embrace of Terrell Jones and Erik Carter.

"Happy Birthday!" they said in unison, each giving him a kiss on the cheek.

"Thanks boys," Dean said, before turning back to Moose. "See, that is how you greet someone. A simple hug and kiss."

Moose was just about to respond, but Dean had already turned away. Terrell and Erik used the opportunity to lick Dean's face down one side and back up the other. Everyone laughed again, as Dean just sighed and reached for another pile of napkins.

Finally, Dean found himself in the arms of the third couple he was dining with, Kurt Peterson and Bill Drake. Bill kissed Dean on one cheek seconds before Kurt planted a very passionate kiss on Dean's lips. His initial embarrassment from Kurt's intense display of affection quickly gave way to a feeling of unconcealed lust.

"Ahem," Moose said.

After getting no response, he finally grabbed Dean and Kurt by the back of their necks and forced them to come up for air. Suddenly the embarrassment was back, especially when he realized that Bill didn't seem all that thrilled with the kiss that his husband had just given him. Everyone knew that Kurt and Bill sometimes brought outside playmates into their relationship, and there had always been a strong flirtation between Kurt and Dean. Less so between Bill and Dean, but there was still some level of attraction there. In all of the years that they had known each other, none of them had ever seriously considered acting on their impulses. But lately, with Dean permanently encamped in Chicago, Kurt seemed to have become much more determined in his quest to get him into their bed.

As Dean prepared himself for what was certain to be a very disapproving comment from Moose, the hostess came up and informed them that their table was ready.

"Saved by the bell," Kurt whispered. He took Dean's hand with his left hand while simultaneously wrapping his right arm around Bill's waist and quickly shuffled them behind the hostess to their table.

As soon as they reached the table, Moose realized that his dinner reservation had been screwed up.

"There are only six seats," he said to the hostess, who looked at him with eyes that were as vacant as they were beautiful.

Sensing that she couldn't quite do the arithmetic required to analyze the problem, Moose pointed out the obvious. "There are seven of us. The reservation was for seven people at seven o'clock. I was very clear."

The next several minutes were a symphony of logistical mismanagement as the hostess, a waiter, and a busboy tried to find an extra chair and place it at a table that was obviously not meant to accommodate seven people. All the while, they were trying to squeeze between and around the other tables and the people in Dean's party, who were doing their best to stay out of the way and failing miserably.

To the gratitude of the other diners, Dean finally took a seat in the newly added seventh chair that was placed awkwardly at the head of the table as everyone else deposited themselves around him.

"You know, this would have been a lot easier if you weren't here," the waiter quipped. Then he was off to get an extra place setting.

It was meant as a joke, and everyone laughed, including Dean. But deep down, on a level that took him by surprise, the comment hit him like a ton of bricks.

The rest of the dinner passed as special events with his friends always did; with much laughter, much teasing, and a lot of love. They drank a bit too much, toasting his advancing years, their longstanding friendships, and absent friends. There were stupid gifts, dirty cards, and enough double entendres to fill a week's worth of bad sitcoms.

But for Dean, there was an uncomfortable feeling that he couldn't shake. He had reached a point in his life where everything should be good and right and happy, but it wasn't. The waiter's comment wouldn't leave his thoughts and he didn't know why. Then, as they were all working their way through his birthday cake, it hit him.

He had somehow become an extra in his own life.

CHAPTER 2

The fact that he was extremely hung over, slightly depressed, and generally in an all-around pissy mood, didn't prevent Dean from being at his desk the following morning for his usual seven AM start to the day. Everyone knew that he was a workaholic and control freak, and he didn't even bother to deny it anymore. He was constantly teased about it, but after awhile he decided that those characteristics that some people might perceive in a negative way were what had allowed him to overcome so many things in his life. They were what had enabled him to become so successful. The were also, in those moments when he allowed himself to dwell on it, part of the reason it was so hard to let someone in to his well-ordered, over-planned life.

As he looked at the stack of papers on his desk, he realized that he should have gone home after his dinner party had ended. Instead, he and his friends had embarked on a birthday bar crawl that hadn't ended until the wee hours of the morning. The whole adventure was made worse by the fact that at each bar his friends felt compelled to tell the bartenders that it was his birthday, which led to far too many tequila shots over the course of the long night.

And then there was Kurt. As they moved from bar to bar, Kurt never left Dean's side. He had obviously wanted to take Dean home with them last night. Dean was amazed that he had actually said no as they were all finally saying their goodbyes and heading their separate ways. Of course, saying no was made a lot easier by the fact that Moose and Peter had been pulling Dean down the street towards their car. For whatever reason, he was finding it increasingly difficult to resist Kurt's advances. He knew that it was probably a bad idea, but whenever he felt Kurt's arms around him, he felt so safe and loved. It had been so long since he had felt those feelings, and he missed them more than he ever thought he would.

Just as his thoughts were about to turn his bad mood into a full blown pity party, his phone rang. Recognizing the phone number on the caller ID, he answered the phone without preamble.

"Hello and thank you so much for the tongue bath you had Moose deliver last night," Dean said.

"Oh, DeeDee, you really must lighten up," Lonny said, using the pet name he had given Dean so many years ago. "One would think that someone as old as you would have learned to take life a bit less seriously."

Lonny Turnow and Dean had met almost thirty years ago, when they were in the sixth grade. Two years later, during a cliché ridden camping trip, they helped each other discover the joys of gay sex. The sex stopped shortly thereafter, and they never brought it up again – until their junior year in college when they came out to each other. After college, they both moved to Chicago. They survived the weather, boyfriends, lovers, the death of Dean's mother, HIV, and sometimes, each other.

Then, a year ago, Lonny got a cough that wouldn't go away. Dean finally forced him to see a doctor. The diagnosis of lung cancer was a shocking as it was improbable. Lonny hadn't smoked a day in his life and was only thirty-five at the time. He fought the disease with the help of his friends, but eventually he couldn't take care of himself and returned to Florida to live with his parents. The best doctors at the Mayo Clinic in Jacksonville and the Cancer Center at the University of Florida were doing everything they could for him, but it was a losing battle. They both knew it, but they rarely talked about it.

"Did you get the check?" Dean asked. "I'm sorry it was so late, but things here have been a bitch lately."

"Yes, Daddy Warbucks, I got the check. I wish you wouldn't worry so much about me getting the check on time. It's not like I have rent to pay."

"I know, but sometimes I stay awake at night wondering if you will have enough money for your Lane Bryant shopping sprees. It worries me to no end," Dean joked.

He had been supporting Lonny for years, even before the cancer. While Dean had always worked too hard, Lonny had taken a very different path. He always held some job or another, but he spent most of his time enjoying life. Dean actually admired him for that, and never really begrudged him the money that he gave him. Especially not now.

"So, how was the birthday dinner? Did they have to help you out of your chair when you needed to go potty? It must be hard to be so many years older than me," Lonny said.

When they were kids, Dean would torment Lonny during the three months before Lonny's January birthday when Dean was numerically two years older. Now, as they were approaching forty, the tables had turned and it was Lonny's turn to do the teasing.

"Well, the evening would have gone a bit more smoothly if I hadn't been there," Dean said before relating the incident with the chairs.

"Oh, I can see where this is going," Lonny said with a sigh. "Let me guess. You have taken this as some sort of sign that you don't belong and you're an outcast and they really didn't want you there and no one loves you."

"You don't know me," Dean muttered. Of course, no one on earth knew him better than his oldest friend and he had hit the nail on the head. "I'm starting to think that I did it all wrong, Lonny. I spent so many years working and traveling, and for what? While I was gone, all of my friends became couples and started building their own lives."

"The bastards! How dare they go out and fall in love. But if memory serves, you've had your opportunities to settle down. In fact, with some of the very same people you're complaining about now."

"I know, I know. But with my job, I was never around enough to do anything about it. Now that I am, I'm wondering if it might be too late."

"Jesus Christ, Dean, you're only thirty-eight years old. It's not like you're never going to meet anyone else. You really have to let go of all these regrets you have. I mean look at your life. You have a great job, you're secure financially, and once I'm dead you'll probably even be able to afford a house."

"That's not funny, Lonny. You know that I don't mind giving you money. I never have. Taking care of you is more important than owning a stupid house," Dean said, not appreciating the morbid joke at all.

"All I'm saying is that you've put your life on hold for too long. And don't give me this bullshit that it was all because of work. It's time for you to start making a life for yourself. Find someone you care about. Spend time with your friends. Be happy. Stop worrying so much about what you've missed and start thinking about what you can do with your life," Lonny said. He was one of the few people who could cut completely through Dean's crap and get to the heart of whatever might be bothering him.

"I'm lonely, Lonny." And that was the simple, unadorned truth. "Even last night, when I was with the guys, I still felt like I was alone."

"I know sweetie, but you can fix that. Did it ever occur to

you that if you put half as much effort into your personal life as you did your professional life, you might be a whole lot happier?"

"Oh you and your silly logic," Dean said with a sigh. Deciding that Dean had probably had enough lecturing for so early on a Friday morning Lonny changed the subject. "So what are you up to this weekend, and don't tell me you're working."

"Well..." Dean started to explain, before being immediately cut off.

"Oh my god, it's like you never listen to me. What did I just say?"

"Relax, please. Yes, I need to get some work done this weekend, but you'll be pleased to hear that I'm also going to be sociable and meet the boys out at Sidetrack tomorrow night. We haven't done that in ages. It should be fun," Dean said, although his voice clearly lacked enthusiasm.

"Sidetrack? Shouldn't you guys be hanging out at Gentry by now?" Lonny joked.

Sidetrack was the most popular gay bar in Chicago, with its massive video screens and multitudes of gorgeous bartenders drawing huge crowds most nights. Gentry, by contrast, was a more sedate piano bar that catered to a somewhat older clientele.

Dean laughed. "You are such a bitch. You were a bitch when I met you and you are a bitch to this day."

"I know," Lonny replied, perfectly happy with the characterization. "Its part of my never ending charm."

"I'm sorry, the connection on your cell phone must be bad, because I thought you just called yourself charming and I have about thirty years of evidence to the contrary."

"Oh my gosh, you are so funny! You know if the connection is bad, maybe you should buy me a new phone. You got me this one almost three years ago. I want a shiny new one. One that I can take pictures of my penis with!"

"Okay, on that rather disturbing note, I need to get ready

for my eight o'clock meeting."

"Who the hell has meetings at eight o'clock on a Friday morning?" Lonny asked. There was such revulsion in his voice that it couldn't possibly have been faked.

"It's my support group for lonely, obsessive-compulsive workaholics," Dean replied. "This morning's meeting topic is 'bitchy friends who just don't understand.'"

Lonny started laughing, which quickly dissolved into a coughing fit from which it took a few moments to recover. Dean's heart sank as he listened to him try to get his deteriorating respiratory system under control.

"Alright, DeeDee, I love you."

"Love you too, and I'm begging you to stop calling me DeeDee," Dean said as he hung up the phone.

He started organizing the papers on his desk to prepare himself for the meeting that was, indeed, fast approaching. As he did, he pushed aside the thought of what his life would be like when the calls from Lonny no longer came.

CHAPTER 3

Dean liked to think that over the years, he'd grown as a person. He liked to think that as the years had passed he'd learned a thing or two about life and grasped some of its meaning. He hoped that he had matured to the point where the shallowness of his youth had been replaced by an appreciation of the truly important things in life. But as he slowly turned and looked at himself in the mirror he was reminded that some things never change and some things, no matter how hard a person tries, are always going to haunt you.

"These jeans make my ass look fat," he said with a sigh.

He knew he wasn't really fat, but far be it for Mr. Self Critical to pass up an opportunity to point out that he wasn't perfect. Standing five feet nine inches and weighing one hundred and seventy pounds, he knew he should probably get to the gym more frequently than his current twice a week schedule. His sandy-blond hair had managed to avoid any gray thus far, and coupled with his round face and good cheekbones managed to give him a boyish look even though he was much closer to forty than he was to thirty. It was a Saturday, so he hadn't bothered to shave, and no one would really be able to tell.

Not quite able to convince himself that he didn't look a little chunky, Dean settled on a linen shirt that looked best when un-tucked, threw on a leather jacket and headed out the door. It was less than a ten minute walk from his apartment on Briar Place to Sidetrack. Arriving shortly after ten o'clock, he found the bar already packed. When he had first moved to Chicago, Sidetrack was a fun little neighborhood bar. Over the years, the bar had consumed storefronts to the north and south of the original establishment, expanding the space in both directions, as well as creating an open air bar in the back and a roof top deck. It was like a big, gay amusement park, with theme nights, no less, and it was usually a lot of fun.

Dean entered the bar and began pushing his way through the tightly packed crowd to the coat check near the back. After dropping off his jacket, he started winding his way back towards the front of the bar, feeling a bit like a salmon trying to make its way upstream. Scanning the crowd, he said a little thank you to do the gods above for making Moose such a giant of a man. Weaving his way in and out of the crowd, using Moose's head as a beacon, he eventually reached his friends, who by the looks of things, been there for some time.

"How is it that you live closer to this place than any of us and yet you're always the last one to get here?" Peter asked.

"All of this doesn't just happen," Dean replied, with a wave to his face. "It takes work."

"Oh sweetie, you might want to consider a different career path," Bill said, drawing a laugh from the crowd.

The truth was that Dean hated being alone in a bar. It had always made him uncomfortable, so he made sure he was one of the last people to arrive whenever he was meeting his friends out.

"Well, I think it was worth the wait," Kurt said. He stepped forward and engaged Dean in their second passionate lip lock of the week.

"Um, *hello!*" Moose yelled over the crowed. He again planted one giant hand on each of their necks and separated them. "Some of the rest of us would like to say hello, you know."

"Hey baby," Dean said. He was forced to stretch up on his tip toes to give Moose a peck on the cheek.

"Hi. Go buy us drinks," Moose said, smiling and tapping his empty beer bottle against Dean's forehead.

"I'll help," Kurt said. He pushed his body behind Dean's and steered him to the bar. Moose, Peter and Bill watched them go, none of them really happy with the flirtation between Dean and Kurt.

"Well, I can see where this night is heading," Bill said to no one in particular.

He watched his husband at the bar laughing with Dean and still plastered to his backside. Bill loved Kurt more than he ever would have thought possible. They were complete opposites physically, but so in tune in almost every other way. Kurt was beefy and dark haired while Bill was blond, lean, and gorgeous. Unfortunately, the things about each other that they both found so attractive made it difficult on those occasions where they wanted to spice up their love life. They could rarely agree on someone to take home.

Bill knew that Kurt had wanted Dean for a long time and he indulged it because Dean never seemed serious about joining them in the sack. Now, things had changed, and it bothered Bill. It wasn't just that he didn't find Dean attractive, because he could get past that. It was the fact that Kurt found Dean *so* attractive. For the first time in their long relationship, Bill began to wonder if this particular three-way might be more than their marriage could handle.

Dean and Kurt returned with beers and vodka slushies for everyone. After relinquishing the drinks, Kurt put his arm around Dean and pulled him close. Bill said nothing, but Moose and Peter could see trouble brewing.

"Oh, look, There's Frank and Gary, let's go say hello," Bill said. He was dragging Kurt away before he even finished the sentence.

"So, are you trying to lose a friend?" Moose asked.

"What? We're just playing," Dean said.

"Kurt isn't playing, Dean," Moose said. "And for god knows what reason, you don't seem to be playing either."

"No offense, Moose, but this is starting to sound a bit hypocritical," Dean said. "You two have been known to share your bed with outsiders every now and then."

"We're also very careful about it. We don't fuck around with friends and we make sure that no one is going to get hurt. You don't have to be a genius to see that Bill doesn't want this to happen," Moose said.

"Wow, this is complicated," Dean said, his words dripping with sarcasm. "So, you can fuck strangers, but friends are off limits? Is there some rule book you could give me so I could create some sort of flow chart that would help me make proper ménage a trois decisions?"

"Considering the number of couples you've slept with, I would have thought you wrote that book," Peter said, coming to his husband's defense.

Dean stared at the two of them, his anger battling with the hurt he was feeling.

"I need another drink," he said, before walking away.

He went back to the bar and fell in line behind the others who were waiting to place their orders. Why did there always have to be so much drama, he wondered? More importantly, who were Moose and Peter to lecture him about fucking around? He was so tired of the hypocrisy, the holier-than-thou attitude they took with him sometimes.

"You look like you need a shot, handsome," the bartender said when Dean finally made his way to the serving area.

"Oh, Terry, I need way more than one," Dean replied. Terry poured him a shot of tequila, which he quickly downed, then went about making Dean's usual vodka-cranberry.

"So, are you ever planning to call me?" Terry asked as he sat Dean's drink on the bar and waved him off when he tried to pay for it.

"I know, I know. I've been so swamped with work that I haven't had time for much of anything lately. I feel terrible that I haven't called you."

"Well, you owe me dinner," Terry said, with a wink. "So give me a call sometime and let's set something up."

"I will, I promise," Dean said, as he grabbed his drink and watched Terry move on to the next customer. They both knew that Dean was never going to call, but it was a game everyone had to play at one time or another.

By the time Dean made his way back to the group, they had been rejoined by Kurt and Bill, who seemed to have made up, or at least they seemed to have agreed to a cease fire.

"Hey sexy, where have you been?" Kurt asked as he again wrapped his arm around Dean.

"At the bar doing shots with Terry and taking a breather from the morality police," Dean said, under his breath.

He was already a little woozy after his first drink and the tequila shot he had at the bar, but he took another gulp of his very strong drink and settled into Kurt's embrace.

Taking in the scene, Moose's anger subsided as he recognized the beginnings of a long night of drinking for Dean. It didn't happen often, but when it did it wasn't pretty. It was as if the only way Dean could let go of being such a control freak was to get wasted.

Changing the subject, and hoping to change the direction of the evening, Moose asked Dean about Terry. "Weren't you two supposed to go on a date a few weeks ago?"

"Yeah, but I had to cancel. My day went long and there just wasn't time. He seems sweet and all, but I don't think I want to reschedule. There's just no spark there."

"You know, you're never going to find a husband if you don't go on the occasional date," Peter said, pointing out the obvious.

"Hey, leave him alone," Kurt said. "Let's not talk about finding him a husband until some of the rest of us have had some fun with him."

"Well, then, maybe we should get it over with, so I can finally settle down with someone," Dean said, giggling as Kurt's hand roamed down his backside.

"Getting if over with sounds fine to me," Bill said. The evening was unfortunately turning out the way he had hoped it wouldn't, but maybe if Kurt got Dean out of his system, they could finally move on.

"Besides, there are all kinds of relationships out there. Ever considered a permanent three-way relationship?" Kurt asked Dean.

"Well, if it means anything, I haven't," Bill said. "Not that I don't adore you, Dean."

Bill was trying to make light of the situation, but he was definitely not enjoying what was happening. In his mind, he tried to do gauge the ramifications of letting Kurt bring Dean home with them. Bill was a financial analyst by trade, and no matter how he sliced this particular equation, he couldn't find an upside.

The rest of the evening was the inevitable disaster that everyone except Kurt and Dean knew it was going to be. Dean continued to drink and Kurt continued to flirt shamelessly with him while Peter, Bill and Moose tried to slow things down. In the end, however, after years of stops and starts, Dean finally went home with Kurt and Bill.

* * * * *

It was after four in the morning, and Dean was still awake. The hours of wild sex that they had engaged in had ended over an hour ago and Kurt and Bill were both sound asleep. Still a little drunk, Dean lay on the far side of the bed, with Kurt behind him and Bill on the other side. That was pretty much how the sex had gone too, he realized. There was definitely something between him and Kurt, but Bill seemed to keep himself at a distance. He wondered how often that occurred. Were Kurt and Bill both always into the third person they brought home or did one of them make some concession when the other one found someone else particularly appealing?

Realizing the utter stupidity of lying in bed several hours before dawn trying to figure out how a couple managed their three-ways, he decided that it was time to go home. He had almost made it out of the bed when he felt Kurt's arm grab him around the waist and pull him back under the sheets.

"Whereyougoing?" Kurt mumbled into Dean's ear. He pulled Dean's body closer to the sensual warmth of his own.

"I'm going to head home," Dean replied, half-heartedly trying to remove Kurt's hand from his chest where it was absently stroking his nipple.

"Stay baby. You feel so good," Kurt sighed, before drifting back to sleep.

Dean knew this was stupid. He knew that tomorrow they would all have breakfast and then Dean would go home alone while Kurt and Bill would go on with their life, together. But the warmth of Kurt's body was so wonderful compared to the empty bed that was waiting for him at home, that he couldn't tear himself away. He reminded himself again that none of this was real. But for one night he decided that he didn't care.

CHAPTER 4

As they did every year, Erik and Terrell hosted a Thanksgiving dinner at their beautiful home in Chicago's Gold Coast. Terrell was that rarest of beasts, a successful artist. His partner, Erik was a lawyer. In addition to having more money than they could ever need, they were both drop-dead gorgeous. Before he began focusing on his trippy modern art paintings, Terrell's striking face and nearly perfect ebony body had graced countless magazines. Erik came from old southern money and a gene pool that included Dixie beauties of both sexes. He had lost everything when his family found out that he was not only gay, but in love with a black man. They say living well is this best revenge. They also say looking great is the best revenge. Either way, Erik had long since moved on from being disowned. It helped that he had practically been adopted into Terrell's Southside family.

Walking into their house was like walking into a HGTV show about five minutes after the team of designers and craftsmen had left, leaving nothing in their wake but room after room of fabulousness. Dean was always amazed by its beauty, and equally amazed that every time he visited, the house looked slightly different. Whether it was Terrell's ever changing art on the walls or Erik's ongoing search for the perfect complimentary antiques, the house always offered a new surprise.

Dean felt a bit of jealously bubbling up and decided that he needed something to head it off at the pass. He had just about reached the bar when he felt a very distinctive, and very large, finger poking him in the back.

In the five days since he had slept with Kurt and Bill, the reality of what he had done had fully settled into Dean's brain. He had used the shortened work week as an excuse to spend as little time as possible talking with his friends because he didn't want to hear the lectures and he didn't want to hear the gossip. But now, with all of them once again gathered together, he knew that he was going to be taking abuse from everyone.

"Hey, sweetie," Dean said, knowing without looking who's finger was pounding into his spine. He turned around and once again started to reach up to give Moose a kiss. Unfortunately, the digit that had been poking him in the back was now firmly planted in the middle of his forehead pushing him back down.

"Why haven't you returned my calls?" Moose asked coldly.

"Oh, you know, just a really busy week," Dean replied, without conviction.

Moose was on the verge of forcefully pointing out how unacceptable that answer was when Peter, sensing that his husband's temper was about to get the better of him, stepped in to save the day, the party, and Dean's ass.

"Now, now children, play nice and we'll let you sit at the grown up table this year," Peter said. Taking pity on Dean, Peter took his husband and guided him toward the bar.

Disaster momentarily averted, Dean moved in the opposite direction toward the nineteenth century sideboard where the appetizers were laid out. Terrell and Erik were standing there, having possibly the gayest discussion humanly possible, regarding the appropriate layout and color distribution of the hors d'oeuvres.

"As much as I hate to interrupt you truckers, I'm starving. What's good?" Dean asked.

"Well, you are, according to Kurt. Bill, however, gave less than stellar reviews," Erik said.

Moose had circled back towards Dean, wine in hand, and laughed an unintentional sonic boom of a laugh upon hearing Erik's comment. The look on Dean's face told everyone that they had crossed the line. Realizing that Moose's earlier interruption had prevented him from reaching the bar, Dean made a beeline for the liquor.

Erik followed Dean and came up beside him. "Look, I'm sorry, that was uncalled for."

"Don't worry about it. I made my bed, so to speak. I guess I'll just have to lie in it. I thought I'd throw that one in before anyone else got a chance."

"Stop it. I said I'm sorry and I promise I'll be good," Erik said. He gave Dean a quick kiss on the cheek and then went back to the sideboard, where Terrell was undoing all of the work that he hand just finished.

Dean watched their playful bickering and felt the familiar pang of jealousy he sometimes felt around them. Dean had briefly dated both of them back in the day. They were both nice and handsome and great to be around, but Dean couldn't make it work with either one of them. But from the moment they had met, Erik and Terrell knew that they were going to be together for the rest of their lives. There had been bumps and bruises along the way, as there always were, but they were happy.

Even as they argued, Dean couldn't help but notice that they were holding hands. What was it about himself that prevented him from finding that kind of comfort with someone else? What was it about all of the couples he knew that allowed them to just be happy with each other and the love they shared and know that it was enough? Whenever Dean was dating someone, no matter how well it began, he eventually started to think that there had to be something more. There had to be stars and rockets and the kind of love that you heard in songs and saw in movies. For a long time, Lonny had told him that he just hadn't met the right guy. But after a number of years he finally told him that he was just too damn picky.

He didn't want to think about couples and romance and lost opportunities. Needing some space, he made his way to the large bay window in the living room that looked out over Dearborn Avenue. It was almost dark out, so even though he was staring out the window, all he could really see was his reflection and the reflection of the guests behind him. He had known he was gay from a very early age and when he was younger and living in a trailer with his mother, he would dream about times like this - living in a big city, surrounded by his gay friends, just being happy to be with each other. Somehow, none of his teenage dreams ever came with this sense of melancholy.

Taking a seat in the large leather chair by the window, Dean gazed out at the crowd that had gathered for the holiday dinner. The strange feeling of disconnect was back and he couldn't figure out how to shake it. He looked at these people that he loved and he came to the conclusion that this was the last place on earth that he wanted to be. He wondered if he were to leave, would anyone notice?

It didn't help matters that Lonny wasn't here. Terrell and Erik had been together for over five years, and every year Dean and Lonny had been coming to their Thanksgiving dinner together. This was the first year that he had been forced to come alone. If Lonny were here he would tell Dean to get over himself and try to have a good time. Instead, he sat and obsessed and nursed his drink.

He had almost succeeded in shaking himself out of his funk when the door opened and the last the guests, Kurt and Bill, arrived. The last *couple*, actually, because Dean had also realized that without Lonny to accompany him, he was the only single person.

Terrell greeted Kurt and Bill and took their coats. Seeing Dean by the window, Kurt immediately made his way over to him. Bill rolled his eyes and watched him go.

"Everything looks beautiful," Bill said, a bit more loudly than was necessary. He was standing by the end of the table which had a single chair, with seven other chairs lined up along each side. "Oh look! There's even a chair for Dean!"

Terrell shot him a look, trying to telepathically warn him that he should tread lightly with Dean.

Bill's comment gave Dean the impetus he needed to get out of the chair and head back to the bar. It was going to be a very long night and he could already see that much more alcohol was going to be required.

"Are you okay?" Moose asked. It never ceased to amaze Dean how someone so large could always manage to sneak up on him.

"Couldn't be better," Dean replied sarcastically. He added a splash of cranberry to the glass that held several shots of vodka. "I'm surrounded by the love and warmth of my wonderful friends. What could possibly be better?"

Moose's earlier anger gave way to the protective feelings he so often felt towards Dean. "Look, I'm sorry about before. And about laughing. It just worries me when you don't return my calls."

"Sweetie, sometimes I just don't feel like talking. Its not that I'm mad or anything, it's just that I need to be alone."

"And sometimes you take that to extremes and we have to send out search parties," Moose said.

It was true that there were periods in his life when he would just drop out, especially if the world was getting to be too much for him. It wasn't anything he planned and he didn't mean anything by it, he just needed to disappear. His friends knew this and absolutely hated it. Several years into his consulting career, while he was working on an assignment in Atlanta, Dean hadn't come home for three consecutive weekends. He also stopped returning calls. Moose had finally called Dean's company and demanded to know where he was. Dean hadn't pulled the disappearing act in years, but still, his friends had long memories. They also loved him, which was really what mattered, he reminded himself.

Moose was like a big puppy dog sometimes and as much as Dean wanted to wallow in every negative emotion he was feeling, he couldn't be mean to Moose. But he didn't want to talk about the shitty evening he was enduring either, so he changed the subject.

"I have some good news," Dean said, forcing himself to appear to be in a better mood, even if he didn't feel it. "Lonny is coming up in a couple of weeks and will be here for your Christmas party."

"That's wonderful! I've missed him so much. How long is he staying?"

"Just for a long weekend. I don't want him to overdo it."

"Sounds fabulous! I can't wait to see him."

Moose put his arm around Dean and walked him towards the table, but not before taking Dean's far too potent drink and putting it back on the bar. They walked over to the table and sat down. Peter joined them, sitting down on the other side of Dean. Ever protective, his two friends.

Everyone gathered at the table, with Bill guiding Kurt to the far end, away from Dean. Erik tapped his glass and stood to make a toast.

"I just want to thank everyone for coming to our home again. Erik and I consider ourselves very blessed to have so many wonderful friends. Now, eat, drink and be nice to one another or so help me god, there will be no pie!"

Everyone cheered and toasted one another and began to dig in to the meal.

The rest of the evening passed without incident and Dean wisely kept his distance from Kurt and Bill. The food was fantastic, the conversation was witty, and the company was good. But Dean could feel that things were changing in his life. He couldn't pinpoint what or why, but he knew that something was wrong. He just didn't know what to do about it.

CHAPTER 5

On Monday afternoon, Dean and Moose had a date for one their frequent lunches. After exiting his office building and heading east on Jackson Boulevard, Dean eventually made his way north on State Street towards Marshall Fields. Of course, it was difficult to keep track of whether or not it still went by the Fields name. Corporate buyouts and the homogenization of the retail industry had long since stripped it of its unique and historic identity. But he had lived in Chicago a long time, and he would always remember this store as it was in its heyday, with the giant iron clocks and hunter green awnings.

Dean had traveled to most of the major cities in the United States, and few could match the beauty of Chicago, even in winter. When he decided to leave the consulting firm, he considered living in other places. He even interviewed for a job in New York. But there was something about Chicago that had a hold on him. It felt comfortable. Even with all of the other feelings he was trying to sort out about his life and his friends, he cherished the comfort of knowing that he lived somewhere that he could truly call home.

One of the best things about not traveling all over the country five days a week was the ability to see his friends more often. Moose, Peter, Erik and Bill all worked in the Loop and they would frequently get together in different configurations depending upon their schedules to catch up on each other's lives.

Moose was waiting for Dean on the seventh floor of Field's, near the food court. As they walked to their usual noodle stand, there was an oddly uncomfortable silence between them.

"Are you mad at me?" Moose asked. For all his bluster and despite his imposing presence, Moose hated it when he wasn't getting along with his friends.

"No, not really. I'm just going through some stuff right now and I'm trying to work a few things out. You know that I can never be really mad at you."

"I know, but it's good to hear."

Moose's mood brightened a bit, but Dean could tell that there was still something on his mind. You should never play poker, big guy, Dean thought.

"So, what's up?" Dean asked, deciding that there was no point in avoiding it further. They had managed to find a table by the windows that overlooked State Street.

"You shouldn't have slept with Kurt and Bill," Moose said.

Dean should have realized that this lecture was coming. He thought that once he made it through the holiday weekend, everyone would have forgotten about his tryst with Kurt and Bill. Or, at the very least, they would have decided that it wasn't anything that anyone needed to worry about.

"Give me break. It was no big deal. We're all big boys and no one got hurt," Dean said.

"Well, that may or may not be true. I talked to Bill, and Kurt really pressured him into sleeping with you. But I'm not talking about them, I'm talking about you. I know that we all play around from time to time, but you seem to have sex with a lot of couples. I'm wondering if there isn't something more to it for you, other than just having fun."

"No offense, honey, but I think your stones are about to break a lot of windows in your little glass house. Its like I said that night at the bar, you and Peter have had more than your fair share of three-ways. Why is it okay for the couple, but the third guy is just some desperate slut?" Dean asked. He hated this double-standard bullshit.

"I'm not saying you're desperate or a slut. I'm just saying that it seems to me that you have sex with more couples than you do single guys. You're getting the reputation as the 'go to' guy for extramarital fucks."

"You mean like you were before you met Peter? Correct me if I'm wrong, but didn't you meet Peter during a three-way with him and his boyfriend at the time? You're hardly the voice of innocence on this topic."

"Is that what you're trying to do? Break up a relationship so that you can snag a husband?" It came out harsher than he wanted it to, but it was out and there was no taking it back.

"I don't need to snag a husband. I'm just fine on my own, thank you very much. Not everyone needs to play by the same rules that you do, Moose. Why don't you let me handle my own love life?"

"The problem is love doesn't really play a role in this, does it? It's just sex, and I think you use it as a way to shield yourself from actually having to think about a relationship and building a life with someone else."

"Spare me the psychoanalysis, Moose," Dean said.

Moose just ignored Dean and plowed ahead. "Furthermore, this isn't just about you. Believe me when I say that Bill was not as into the three-way as you and Kurt were. He sees the way that you two look at each other. It's not easy keeping a relationship together, Dean. Do you really want to be responsible for breaking one up?"

"You have five seconds to change the topic or I'm out of here," Dean said.

"Fine. I think its time you started going out alone, instead of always hanging out with couples."

"For fuck's sake!" Dean exploded, and then lowered his voice. "Are you trying to piss me off? What on earth is the matter with you today?"

"Nothing is the matter with me. I've wanted to talk to you about this for awhile and I guess now is the time. How do you ever expect to meet someone if you are hanging out with all of us all the time?"

"I didn't know that my company wasn't desired as long as I was single. If I find a boyfriend will you let me sit with you guys in the lunch room?"

"I'm not even going to dignify that with a response. You know we all love you and love being with you. All I'm trying to say is that I really think your life is going to be missing something until you finally meet someone."

It hit him like a punch in the stomach. All of the things that had been bothering Dean for the past few weeks finally coalesced into a clear, and very disturbing, realization.

"I want to thank you for lunch. It's been quite an eye-opener." Dean's anger had reached a point where all emotion had drained from his voice and his face and it scared the shit out of Moose.

"Dean, look..." Moose began, but Dean cut him off.

"No. Seriously, *thank you*. Something has been bothering me lately and it wasn't until just now that I've been able to put my finger on in it. Despite everything you've said about how much you guys love me and how great you think I am, I think the truth is that you all think you're better than me."

"What? That's not what I meant at all," Moose said. He couldn't believe that Dean really thought he was implying that.

"Do you remember a few weeks ago when we were all over at your house for game night? The last thing we played was that bitchy *True Colors* game," Dean said.

"Of course, I thought we all had a great time."

"Right," Dean said, sarcastically. "One of the questions

during the game was something like 'In High School, which of the players was probably voted most likely to succeed – but didn't?' You know, that was the only question that had a unanimous verdict. Me. You all voted for me. And I'm wondering why that is? Is it because I don't own my own home? Because I'm single? Because I'm leech trying to break up marriages so that I can snag a husband? What is it about me that makes my friends think I'm such a loser?"

"None of us think you are a loser, honey. We just worry about you, that's all. We want you to be happy."

"Well, you're doing a bang-up job of that today. All your talk about being concerned about me and worrying about my happiness is bullshit. You look down on me. Despite everything I've managed to overcome in my life, you think that you are better than me. Let me tell you something, you know me better than anyone this side of Lonny, but you don't know everything about me. You don't know what I've been through, you don't know what is going on in my life and you don't know what makes me happy."

"And whose fault is that? You're so tightly wound, so in control of everything, you never let anyone in. Maybe if you leaned on people a bit more we would understand you a bit better."

"Judging by this conversation, the only thing opening up to my friends would do is give them more reasons to think less of me. Again, thanks for lunch, it sucked."

With that, Dean got up and walked away and Moose realized that he had gone too far.

* * * * *

Ten minutes later, Dean was sitting on a bench in Millennium Park, staring at his distorted figure in the shiny "bean" sculpture that served as the park's icon. He couldn't go back to work right away because he was too angry – at both Moose and himself. Staring at the bean wasn't helping, so he ventured into the park and began walking slowly south toward his office.

It pissed him off how condescending Moose had been. He hated it when people, even the people who loved him, thought they knew what was best for him. It wasn't so much that Moose had offered up opinions on what Dean needed to do in order to make his life better; it was the fact that he did it without even talking to him about it. 'Oh, I've thought about it, Dean, and if you just do this, this and this, you'll be so much happier.'

Even worse was that it all centered on Dean being single. Who was Moose to tell him that he needs to stop hanging out with couples or he's never going to meet anyone? What business is it of his? How dare he assume that he wasn't happy with his life just the way it was. Admittedly, he knew that he wasn't all that happy with the current state of his life, but the notion that married people knew so much better than single people the key to happiness was so patently false it drove him crazy.

He had wandered past the open air amphitheater and crossed back towards the park's fountains. He was getting odd looks from the tourists and realized that he had probably been mumbling to himself. Continuing south, he crossed the street and wandered into the small park on the grounds of the Art Institute. He'd always loved this little park, almost as much as loved the museum itself.

He sat quietly, closed his eyes and took a few deep breaths. As his head began to clear, he realized that he might be overreacting a bit. True, he was pissed at Moose for what he had said, but there was a part of him that realized his anger was coming from the fact that he had hit a little too close to home.

Dean had never been one of those people that needed a man in his life in order to be fulfilled. Still, he couldn't deny the appeal of having someone who was always there for you, having someone to share things with, of having someone to lean on. But he had been alone for so many years that he had long since reconciled himself to the fact that a relationship couldn't be the Holy Grail for him. He would find a way to be happy, with or without someone by his side, regardless of whether or not his friends thought that was possible.

CHAPTER 6

Dean nursed his coffee and leaned against a wall at the far end of the gigantic concourse that housed the baggage claim at O'Hare International Airport. Looking at the thousands of people coming and going, he was struck once again by how happy he was that he no longer had to deal with this madness week after week. He had positioned himself so that he could see the arrival screens. A quick check showed that Lonny's flight was still ten minutes from landing.

God, how he had missed Lonny. It was hard to believe that they had known each other almost thirty years. They had first met several months after Dean's father had been killed. The first of so many losses, he now knew. Dean's childhood was very clearly defined as the time before his father died and the time after his father died. Before his father died, times were tough. After he died, they were much worse.

Dean's parents had met in high school in Scranton, Pennsylvania. Andy and Becky were inseparable and married right after they graduated. Neither of them was college bound, so they started working in Andy's brother's diner. They had often talked about opening their own restaurant, but they figured it would be years before they had the money to make that leap. Two years after they married, Dean was born and Becky left the restaurant to take care of him. From the pictures that Dean had seen over the years, they looked like a typical young family. They looked happy. They never had a lot of money, but that didn't seem to matter much. Dean loved both his parents and had nothing but good memories of his early childhood.

Despite the lack of money, Dean's parents found ways to make sure something special happened every now and then; an extra special birthday present here, a weekend in Atlantic City or Philadelphia there. It was never anything huge, but they always managed to make it memorable. His fondest memory of his father, really the last great memory of him, occurred during spring break when Dean was in the fifth grade. He and his father went camping. Just the two of them. Catching their dinner, cooking fish over an open fire, sleeping in the tent together, listening to the sounds of the forest during the night. It all seemed so magical to him. There were times, in the years that followed, when Dean wished that he didn't have those memories because the ache they caused broke his heart all over again.

Then, as if someone had flipped a switch, his life changed. He was setting the table for dinner one steamy July afternoon when his Aunt Jo and Uncle Walt came in through the back door. Dean continued setting the table, with no reason to think anything was amiss because members of his extended family often stopped by whenever they felt like it. He had just put his father's plate down when he heard his mother scream. He ran into the kitchen to find his aunt holding her and comforting her. His uncle grabbed Dean by the shoulders and sat him down to explain what had happened, but Dean didn't hear anything after 'Son, your father's been killed.'

His father had been less than a block away from the restaurant when a drunk driver ran a red light and plowed into his car. The drunk walked away without a scratch, but Andy was killed instantly. Something inside Dean's mother died that day too, but he wouldn't realize that for a couple of years.

Two weeks later, his mother came in to his room and told him that she had decided that they were going to move to Florida. His grandparents had retired to the small city of St. Augustine several years before and she wanted to live near them. She needed to go back to work and was going to need help taking care of Dean. He told his mother that he understood. After she left his room, he cried for hours before finally falling asleep.

In mid-August they moved into a small trailer in the trailer park where his grandparents were living. Dean hated it. He hated the people who lived there, he hated the weather and the mosquitoes, he hated his mother for moving him there, and he hated his father for dying.

When junior high started in the fall, things weren't any better. Dean had no way of relating to his redneck classmates. It wasn't until a month later that things finally changed for him. He was sitting in the cafeteria, alone as usual, when Lonny came up and sat down across from him. For whatever reason, Lonny had decided to befriend him. He started talking and drawing Dean out of his shell. And that was that. From that moment on they were best friends. Looking back, he realized that Lonny had probably saved his life.

Dean forced his mind away from the past. He knew those memories were not what he needed right now, so he set them to the side in his mind, an ability he had picked up long ago. He walked over to a garbage can to throw away his empty coffee cup. Looking up he saw a man who looked like a nightmare version of Lonny coming towards him. Dean's heart sank when he realized that it *was* Lonny. The cancer had started to take a toll before he had left Chicago, but it wasn't so bad that you would notice it without really looking for it. Now, however, it was everywhere. He had probably lost twenty pounds since Dean had last seen him. His clothes hung on him like an under-stuffed scarecrow. His face had aged ten years and his hair had turned a lifeless color. Realizing that Lonny had not yet seen him, he buried his shock and walked towards him until his friend finally saw him.

"Hey you," Dean said, gently wrapping him in a hug. "God, I've missed you."

"I've missed you too sweet cheeks. Okay, get off me, you're crushing me."

Dean pulled back and looked at his old friend. Lonny used the moment of silence as an opportunity to say what he had been waiting nine hundred miles and three hours to say.

"Why are you fighting with Moose?"

"That's it, I'm canceling your cell phone," Dean said.

* * * * *

After an agonizing forty-five minute cab ride, they finally arrived at Dean's apartment. Lonny had not let up about Moose during the entire trip. Now, to add insult to injury, he was continuing his harangue as Dean carried his suitcase up the three flights of stairs to his apartment. Dean had just about reached his limit when he realized that Lonny had stopped talking, and had stopped walking up the stairs altogether for that matter. Turning around, he saw Lonny leaning against the wall trying to catch his breath.

"Are you okay?" Dean asked, his suddenly intense concern erasing every trace of annoyance he had been feeling.

"Just a bit winded," Lonny replied. "It's been awhile since I've had to deal with stairs. Don't think for a minute that this is going to allow you to change the subject."

"Oh, I'm sorry, were you talking about something?"

After they entered the apartment, Lonny plopped himself down on the couch while Dean took the suitcase into his bedroom. When he came back to the living room, he noticed that Lonny still looked drained from the walk up the stairs.

"Do you want some tea or something?" Dean asked.

"No, I'm fine. Come and sit down for a minute, I want to talk to you about something."

"Seriously, Lonny, I don't want to talk about Moose anymore. It was a fight. I'm sure we'll make up at some point. But I really am tired of hearing about it."

"DeeDee, come sit down for a minute," Lonny said. His voice had taken on a much different tone, so Dean sat down next to him and waited.

"I'm dying, Dean," Lonny said simply.

"Sweetie, I know things haven't been going so well, but I talked to your Mom last week and she told me that you were meeting with a doctor at the Mayo Clinic to talk about a new treatment. What did they say?"

"It's a very invasive treatment, and it's not a cure. It just prolongs things. I'd be hospitalized for the better part of three months, and I just can't put myself through that. I'm tired, Dean."

"What are you saying?"

"I'm saying that I've fought the good fight, but I'm done. This is going to be hard for you to understand, but you reach a point where it just doesn't make sense to go on fighting. I've been in pain for almost two years now, and I'm exhausted. I never thought that anyone could be so tired. There are times when I wake up in the middle of the night crying because of the pain. It's just been too much for too long."

"Lonny..."

"I had a long talk with my parents and my doctors and we're all in agreement. I'm still taking medications to ease the pain, but other than that, I'm done. I'm just letting nature take its course now."

"What you're doing is giving up. This is bullshit! I don't want to sound like a bad movie, but where there's life, there's hope. You've got to believe that things will get better."

Dean had jumped up from the couch and was pacing the living room. He couldn't believe what he was hearing.

"Honey, I could spend the next few hours talking to you

about my medical history and everything we've tried and everything that hasn't worked, but I think it's just easier for me to say that you're going to have to trust me - we have looked at this from every possible angle. Some treatment or another might put the inventible off for a few months, but I am going to die. I'd rather live the next few months the best that I can than another year in constant pain. Either way, the same end result is going to occur."

"Months? This isn't happening," Dean said, stunned by what Lonny was telling him.

Lonny stood up and walked over to Dean, who instinctively pulled away. All these years, Lonny thought, and he still wouldn't let people get close to him, even the people who loved him the most.

"Its okay, DeeDee. It really is going to be okay."

Dean just stood there, allowing himself to be hugged. A normal person would have cried, but Dean just didn't have it in him. He couldn't cry because that would mean acknowledging the truth about what he was hearing, and he wouldn't do that. He had lost so many people over the years, but this was too much. He couldn't conceive of a world that Lonny wasn't a part of. So he did the only thing he could do – he hugged his oldest, dearest friend as if his own life depended on it.

CHAPTER 7

On Saturday night, Dean and Lonny made their way north to Andersonville for Moose and Peter's Christmas party. Before leaving, Lonny warned Dean to put his argument with Moose behind him. He decided not to tell Dean that he agreed with Moose because that would have led to an entirely new argument, and he wanted to enjoy the evening.

As the cab sped north along Lake Shore Drive, Lonny was flooded with memories of his life in Chicago. When he and Dean had moved to the city, they really had no idea what to expect. It had turned out to be more than either of them could have hoped for. Over the years they had made so many friends and had so many good times that he truly felt he could leave the world with no regrets. Well, except that he would have liked more time. And he wished that there were someone to look out for Dean. He couldn't do much about time, but he had a plan in mind to take care of Dean.

When the reality of his cancer had settled in and he finally came to grips with how little time he had left, it wasn't himself or his family that he was most concerned about, it was Dean. They had always been there for each other, through everything that had happened in their lives, and he was afraid of what would become of Dean once he was gone. He hadn't mentioned that part of the reason for this trip was so that he could make sure that their Chicago friends were going to be there for Dean after he was gone.

"Penny for your thoughts," Dean said, shaking Lonny from his reverie.

"Hmmm? Oh, I was just thinking how much I have missed everyone."

"Are you planning on telling them?"

"No. Somehow I don't think Miss Manners would approve of announcing my impending death smack in the middle of a Christmas party. That's between you and me, for now."

They drove the rest of the way in silence. When they reached Moose and Peter's house, Dean could see Lonny visibly brighten. The house was decorated extensively for Christmas and the windows blazed with light in the cold night air. For his part, Dean had never felt as comfortable anywhere as he did at Moose and Peter's. Everything was nice, but nothing was overdone. Their house, more than even Lonny's parents' house, felt like home to Dean. It exuded warmth and love. He envied Moose and Peter for the life they had built together.

After making their way inside, he and Lonny were taking off their coats when Dean noticed Moose, Peter, Kurt and Bill chatting near the fireplace. There was a brief moment of silence as everyone took in the sight of Lonny, who looked almost nothing like they remembered. Dean took Lonny's arm and led him to their friends and began a round of hugs and kisses. His kiss to Kurt was, again, longer than necessary and his hug to Moose was colder than it should have been. Lonny followed Dean in the mini-reception line and noticed how delicately everyone hugged him, as if they were afraid he might break. When all the greetings had been exchanged, the uncomfortable silence again fell over the group.

"Oh, for fuck's sake! I feel like Debra Winger in *Terms of Endearment*. Tell everyone its okay to talk about the cancer!" Lonny said, doing a very poor impersonation of the actress' husky voice. Everyone laughed, and the years that bound them together melted away.

"Actually, we were all just waiting with baited breath to see if Moose and Dean were going to bare their claws again," Peter said.

"What's going on with you two?" Kurt asked, unaware that he was the reason for their falling out.

"Nothing major," Moose said, glaring at Peter.

"Um, who wants a drink?" Peter asked.

Everyone moved to the kitchen, but Kurt held Dean back. Lonny tried to stay, but Kurt shooed him away. Lonny gave Dean a look of warning before following the rest of the group into the kitchen.

"What was that all about?" Kurt asked as he wrapped his arms around Dean.

Dean laughed a small, bitter laugh. "Apparently when I slept with you and Bill, I set the wheels of Armageddon in motion."

"Oh, whatever. They're all just jealous." Kurt kissed him deeply and Dean couldn't help but respond. Finally, he pulled away.

"Speaking of jealous, Moose tells me that Bill wasn't so thrilled with the three of us getting it on. The last thing I want to do is cause trouble between you two."

"I'm not sure what Bill's problem is lately. It's not like we haven't been doing this for awhile now. But lately, he seems to be irritated by it rather than just having fun."

"Then maybe it's time for you to slow down a bit."

"Maybe so, but then I wouldn't get to be with you again."

They both knew they were playing with fire, and they both knew that it would probably end badly. Still, there they were, once again flirting up a storm.

What exactly do I want out of this? Dean wondered to himself. Before he could worry too much about it, a drink was thrust between his and Kurt's faces.

"Drink?" Lonny asked. It was amazing how one little word could be so easily translated into 'you two seriously need to get the fuck away from each other.'

Kurt laughed and ambled toward the kitchen while Lonny guided Dean to the couch.

"You've got to be kidding me with this, Dean."

"Leave it alone, Lonny. I don't want to argue about this with you, too. Besides, I'm pretty sure that the three of us aren't going to go down that road again anytime soon."

"*Pretty sure* doesn't fill me with confidence," Lonny replied.

They sat on the couch and looked around the crowded room. "Anyway, enough of that. Let's gossip. What have I missed since I've been gone?"

Dean took in the guests and realized that there wasn't much to tell. "You know, you haven't missed much. It's the same people that you've always known. They're all in the same place in their lives that they were when you left. Nothing's really changed."

"Okay, sunshine, what on earth is the matter with you?"

"I wish I knew. I really do. I thought that once I stopped with all the travel and I was with everyone all the time, things would be different. I don't know what I was expecting, but it wasn't this. I still feel, I don't know, like I don't belong."

"Well, honey, you've always been a bit of a loner, and it had nothing to do with your travel schedule. Its part of who you are. I'm not saying it's a good thing or a bad thing, but it is you. Were you expecting a personality transplant just because you were in the same area code all the time?"

Dean laughed softly. Lonny had a point. He had never been the most outgoing person. His shyness had always forced him somewhat into the background. It was only when others like Lonny or Moose drew him out of his shell that he really started interacting with people.

"I sometimes think that I'm really messed up in some way," Dean said. "Look around this room. Look at all of the couples. Look at all the friends. I mean, are they really as happy as they seem? Is there something they know that I don't know? What it is about me that prevents me from opening myself up to a boyfriend, to my friends, to anybody?"

"Well, we can sit here brooding about why you never seem to join in the fun, or we could, you know, get off our asses and go join in the fun."

"Leave it to you to concoct a perfectly simple plan and ruin a wonderful bout of self-loathing," Dean said, as he helped Lonny up off the couch.

Dean went over to talk to Peter and Erik, while Lonny excused himself and went to get another drink. The evening was slowly getting better and Dean forced himself to relax and just enjoy the company of his friends. He even managed to make up with Moose, as he always did. The truth was, only someone who loved him as much as Moose did could get under his skin the way he had. Deep down he knew that Moose was trying to look out for him, even if he didn't do it in the most graceful way possible.

Over the next few hours, Dean and Lonny made their way from one group of friends to the next. Around eleven, they got separated and Dean was forced to endure a conversation between Terrell and Peter about the merits of performance art. As his eyes began to glaze over, he noticed Lonny and Moose involved in a deep conversation in the kitchen. He excused himself and made his way over to them. They noticed him as he approached and immediately stopped talking about whatever it was they had been discussing.

"What are you two old ladies up to?" he asked.

"Nothing, just chatting a bit," Lonny said.

"It didn't seem like nothing," Dean said, eyeing them suspiciously.

"I was telling Moose that the party is wonderful, but I think it's time for me to go home. I'm not used to this glamorous lifestyle anymore. You should stay, though. I'll just hop in a cab."

"Don't be silly. I'll go with you."

"No, stay and have fun. It's early."

"Lonny, I'm not putting you in a cab and sending you home. I'll go home with you. I'm actually kind of tired."

The argument went back and forth for several minutes before they realized that Moose had walked away, retrieved both of their coats, returned, and was standing in front of them, waiting patiently.

"Okay, Chip and Dale, this could go on all night, so I thought it best if I just decided that you should both leave. I've known you guys long enough to know how this is going to end."

Dean and Lonny laughed and accepted their coats. They began the slow trek from one end of the house to the other, saying their goodbyes. Dean decided that discretion was definitely the better part of valor and gave Kurt a quick peck on the check. Bill managed to look grateful and wary at the same time. Kurt, who was a bit tipsy, was about to demand a much more meaningful goodnight kiss when Lonny stepped between them and gave him a very definitive good night.

Moose walked them to the door to make sure the cab that he had called was waiting for them.

"The four of us are having lunch tomorrow, yes?" Moose asked.

"Absolutely," Lonny replied. "Call us when you wake up and let us know when you are going to be ready."

"Will do," Moose said.

"And please try to make it sometime around noon," Lonny said. "I can't deal with one of your infamous three pm lunches."

"I'm sure I don't know what you mean," Moose said sweetly.

As Dean was opening the door to leave he turned from

Moose and found himself bumping into one of the most attractive men he'd seen in a very long time.

"Oh god, sorry about that," Dean muttered. He was trying to get out of the way, but all he succeeded in doing was performing his half of the left-right samba that two people who are in each other's way always seem to inflict upon each other.

"Don't worry about it," the stranger said. Finally, he grabbed Dean by the shoulders, held him firmly in place, and then gently stepped around him into the living room.

Dean seemed flustered, which surprised Moose, because he never got flustered.

"Hey gorgeous," Moose said, hugging the man and planting a kiss on his cheek. "I'm so happy you could make it. I want you to meet some friends of mine who, unfortunately, were just leaving. Dean Davenport, Lonny Turnow, this is Tony Finelli."

"Pleased to meet you both," Tony said, as he shook hands with Lonny, then Dean. Tony and Dean's eyes were locked on each other the entire time.

"Nice meeting you too," Lonny said. It seemed clear that Dean had lost his ability to speak. "Dean says it's nice to meet you too, don't you Dean?"

"What?" Dean asked. He suddenly realized that he had been staring at Tony for far too long. "Oh, sorry. Right. Very nice to meet you. I'm Dean."

"I think I got that," Tony said as Moose and Lonny laughed. Dean blushed and Tony decided it was the cutest thing he had ever seen.

The cab's horn blared and Dean and Lonny knew it was time for them to go. As they walked away, the door closed and Dean began to regain his composure. He held the cab door open for Lonny.

"Are you sure you don't want to stay?" Lonny asked. "I think he might have liked you."

"Shut the fuck up and get in the cab," Dean replied, his gruff exterior doing a poor job of masking the effect that meeting Tony had on him. The cab pulled away as Dean looked through the front window and saw Tony being introduced to others at the party. He sighed as the house slowly faded from view.

CHAPTER 8

As absurd as it sounded, there were times when Dean thought that he had given up a very lucrative career so that he could go bowling once a week. That wasn't the only reason, of course, but it had been the trigger. About a year before he left his consulting job, Dean was enjoying a rare week in Chicago. He was between assignments and was spending very little time in the office. Moose had called him and asked him if wanted to be a substitute on their bowling team.

Moose and Peter, Kurt and Bill, along with their friend Luis had been bowling together for about three years. Actually, they had been drinking a lot of beer together for about three years. The bowling was usually incidental. The week Dean was in Chicago, Luis was in Los Angeles for work, something he had been doing with greater frequency. Dean went bowling that night, which planted the seed in his mind that his life might be a lot happier if he spent more time with his friends than he did the staffs at the Hyatt hotels across the country. Shortly after Dean quit his job, Luis relocated to L.A. and

Dean joined the team.

It was the final week of bowling before the holiday break. Much to his own amazement, Dean was not running late. His friends had threatened to feed him through the ball return if he was tardy one more time. Kurt and Bill were already at their assigned lane when Dean arrived.

"Dear God, it's a Christmas miracle!" Bill exclaimed in amazement. "You're actually early. I don't think I know how to deal with you when you're early."

"Shut up and give me a kiss," Dean said, giving Bill and Kurt quick kisses before he began to unload his gear. "I realized at five o'clock I had accomplished all that I needed to do for the day and decided to leave. Things are slowing down a bit before the holidays."

"And they just let you leave?" Bill asked.

"No, I snuck out. I felt dirty," Dean joked.

Not satisfied with a quick peck on the cheek, Kurt wrapped Dean in a hug, his hands groping Dean's ass. "Exactly how dirty do you feel?"

Dean was about to give an equally lewd reply when he caught Bill shaking his head. Wednesday nights were Dean's time to relax, and the last thing he wanted to do was create drama, so he slipped out of Kurt's grasp and headed for the line.

"Not that dirty. Now get out of my way, I need to practice. If I bowl as shitty as I did last week, you guys will never let me live it down."

Kurt gave his husband a mildly annoyed glare, and was about to say something, but just then, Moose and Peter walked in. Thank god, Dean thought, saved by the bears.

"Did Lonny get home okay?" Peter asked, after giving Dean a kiss hello.

"Yeah, we had coffee downtown this morning before he hopped on the Blue Line to the airport. He called me this afternoon to let me know that he was home," Dean said.

"It was so great to see him," Bill said.

"He loved seeing you guys, too. He had a blast at showtunes on Sunday. Although he was a bit drunk on purple slushies by the time we left."

"Well, some things never change," Peter said, with a smile.

"So, I didn't want to ask him, but how is he doing?" Bill asked.

"He's..." Dean began, before stopping himself. What to say? Tell the truth or keep up the pretense? "He could be doing better. Time will tell I suppose."

They all knew Dean well enough to know that that was as close to an emotional outburst has he was likely to get so they let it drop. They had all talked at lunch on Tuesday, which Dean and Lonny had not been able to attend. The consensus was that Lonny probably didn't have much time. They were saddened by the realization, but they were gay men of a certain age and they had all lost friends and lovers over the years. They weren't immune to the feelings of loss that accompanied death, but they were accustomed to them.

Moose, ever the cheerleader, decided that a subject change was in order.

"So, Dean, Tony was asking a lot of questions about you after you left."

"Oh, really?" Dean replied, noncommittal even though his heart seemed to skip a beat at the mention of Tony's name. "What kind of questions?"

"Like, are you single? What do you do? Are you single? Is he your type? Are you single? That kind of thing," Moose said.

"Tony? The guy who came in later in the evening?" Kurt asked. "That guy's a weirdo."

"You don't even know him," Peter said. "You just met him that night."

"I know, but I've heard some things about him and there's just something about him that seems a little off."

"He seemed very nice to me," Bill said. He ignored the annoyed look his husband was once again giving him. "What did you think, Dean?"

The butterflies that Dean had been feeling gave way to a sense of caution as he noticed the tension between Kurt and Bill. Maybe Moose was right, and Bill didn't appreciate what had happened between the three of them.

"He seemed very nice," Dean finally said. It was the chicken-shit way out, but he was determined to get through the evening without any sort of confrontation.

"Oy vey," Moose muttered. "What on earth am I going to do with you? I saw the way you two were looking at each other when you ran into him at the door. There was a definite spark there."

"Spare me the yenta routine, Moose," Dean said. "You're Lutheran for Christ's sake."

"I'm just saying, he's single, *you're* single. You two could go on a date or something. I know a date is like the seventh circle of hell for you, but maybe you should try it more than once or twice a year. You might find that you actually enjoy it."

"And I'm just saying that I'm very busy at work, the holidays are coming up, and I'm going to Florida. Now isn't the best time to start a relationship."

"One date," Peter chimed in. "Just one date. Who said anything about a relationship? Oh, wait a minute – that was you."

Dean was just about to try and dig himself out of the conversation when he was saved by the appearance of their opponents for the evening.

"Hello Ladies!" Corey Levington said with a flourish.

Dean used the greetings between his team and Corey's as a diversion and made his way back to the line to throw another practice ball. Considering how unfocused he was, he wasn't at all surprised when he got a split.

"So, did you boys hear about all the drama? The league lost a team this week," Corey said breathlessly.

"Get out. Who?" Moose asked.

"Well, apparently, the *Balls to the Wall* team was a very

incestuous little group. Aaron and Stan, who have been together forever, had been sleeping with Henry for months. Sunday night, Stan comes home from a weekend in Indianapolis visiting his parents to find that Aaron has cleared all of his stuff out of their house and moved in with Henry!"

"Holy shit," Peter said. "Aaron and Stan have been together longer than we have."

"Wait, it gets better," Corey continued. "So Stan shows up at Henry's house on Sunday night to find out what the hell is going on. Huge fight! The neighbors actually had to call the police. Nobody was arrested, but still, can you imagine!"

"How do you know all of this?" Bill asked.

"One of the other guys on the team called me on Monday morning and gave me the entire blow-by-blow, so to speak. Turns out that Aaron told Stan that he had fallen in love with Henry and they wanted to build a life together. Just the two of them."

"Wow. I guess that is the risk you take when you bring someone into your relationship," Moose said, with all the subtlety of a wrecking ball.

Waiting for his ball to come back, Dean studiously ignored Moose and everyone else. The gossip continued on behind him and he blocked it out. He fidgeted by the ball return wondering if the ancient machinery had made a meal of his bowling ball.

Dean noticed Michael Stanton was subbing on Corey's team this evening. He and Michael had flirted on and off for years before finally going on a date about six months ago. The dinner was great, the conversation was wonderful, and the sex was pretty damn good too, as Dean recalled. Michael, being a normal, red-blooded gay man, had asked Dean out for a second date. Dean, being Dean, declined. He let him down as gently as he could, considering he couldn't really come up with a reason why he didn't want to go out with him again. Michael had been hurt, but had moved on and had been dating one of Corey's teammates for almost four months.

Dean's ball shot up through the chute and he went back to

the line to try and pick up the spare. How many guys like Michael were there in his past? How many guys like Erik and Terrell? How many perfectly good guys had he gone out with once or twice before deciding that there wasn't enough there to continue seeing them? More importantly, how many of those guys did he now look back on with regret? Why didn't he try harder? Every time someone got close, he found something wrong with them and pushed them away. Why couldn't he figure out a way to keep a romance going? To let someone in? To just be a normal guy dating another normal guy? Why did he insist on being alone?

"Um, are you planning on throwing the ball anytime soon, sweetie?" Moose asked from behind Dean.

"Sorry," Dean replied. He was just about to throw the ball when he turned back to look at Moose. "So Tony was asking about me, huh?"

Moose just smiled. But inside, the wheels were turning.

CHAPTER 9

A week and a half later, Dean was once again on the northbound Red Line train, this time heading to Kurt and Bill's house for what was, thankfully, the last Christmas party before he left for Florida. He loved his friends, he loved the parties, and he loved the holidays, but after a few weeks it got to be a bit too much.

The snow had begun to fall heavily and he was grateful beyond words for Chicago's mass transit system. He had never owned a car in Chicago, and he didn't have any plans to change that. On nights like this, just trying to find a parking space could take upwards of half an hour. Then, after whatever party or dinner or event you were attending was over, you got to dig out of the snow and try to drive home without getting into an accident. Once there, you got to spend yet another half hour finding parking, which wouldn't be remotely near where you lived. You just had to make sure that parking was allowed on that particular street when snow was falling. In the alternative, you could avoid the street parking hassle altogether and park in the comfort of your own building for two hundred dollars a month. It was such a racket.

Still, he knew that of all of his friends, he was the only one taking the train tonight. Everyone else drove their nice cars, from their nice homes or condos and then back again. Whenever a trip out of the city came up that required driving, someone always had to pick Dean up. No one ever complained, but it always bothered him. He always felt like something of a burden.

There were times when he looked around at all his friends had and all they had accomplished and he wondered if the choices that he had made over the course of his life were so bad that they had led him to a point where he was always going to be a step behind everyone else? Or were the cards stacked against him from the beginning? Dean shook himself out of his thoughts as the train pulled in to the Bryn Mawr station. He trotted down the steps and began the short walk to Kurt and Bill's house.

Even though he didn't have far to go, he was covered in snow by the time he reached the party. He was standing on the front porch, shaking off the snow, when Moose and Peter came walking up the path to the house - along with Tony.

"Hey, handsome," Peter called out.

"Hello boys," Dean said. "You guys look like Frosty the Gay Snowmen. Where did you end up parking?"

"Do *not* ask," Moose grumbled. "But the long walk was worth it. Look who we found along the way. You remember Tony?"

"Of course. Nice to see you again," Dean said, shaking Tony's hand and again feeling that electricity that he felt the first night they met, even through their gloves.

"You too," Tony replied. As he let go of Dean's hand, he reached up and wiped the last bit of snow out of Dean's hair, and then straightened it.

"Thanks," Dean said. He was praying that they would all think that it was the cold that had made his cheeks turn red.

Just then the door opened and Kurt was there to greet them.

In the space of two seconds he managed to smile when he saw Moose and Peter, smile even broader when he saw Dean, and deflate just a bit when he saw Tony.

"What on earth are you guys doing out here?" Kurt asked, as he herded them inside. "Oh, god, I'm gonna be so hung over when I shovel that crap in the morning."

Once inside, Bill appeared and helped Kurt take their coats and the various gifts and bottles of wine they had brought for their hosts. He was also very happy to see Dean standing next to Tony, however that had managed to occur.

"Thanks for inviting me," Tony said to Kurt, as he handed him his coat. "It was a nice surprise."

"It's a surprise for me too," Kurt said dryly. He was trying to make a joke, but it failed miserably.

"Oops, that's my bad," Bill said. "Peter called today and mentioned that Tony didn't have any plans for this evening so I told him the more the merrier."

"Absolutely! Drinks are in the kitchen, food is in the dining room. Go dig in," Kurt said, as he tried to hide his displeasure with his husband.

The group started snaking their way toward the kitchen, with Bill leading the way and Dean bringing up the rear. Unfortunately, like the slowest gazelle on the Serengeti, that made him easy pickings for the nearest predator. Kurt grabbed him with the arm that wasn't loaded down with coats and planted a passionate kiss on his lips.

"Umm, come help me with the coats."

Bill just sighed and continued leading everyone else to the kitchen. He wasn't sure if they were ready for a drink but he knew that he sure as hell needed one.

In the bedroom, Kurt threw the coats on the bed and then threw Dean down on top of the coats. They kissed deeply and passionately. Dean was very uncomfortable for two big reasons, first because he didn't want Bill or one of the guests walking in and second, he was pretty sure someone's cell phone was lodged up his ass.

"Have I ever told you what an amazing kisser you are?" Kurt asked.

"Years of practice," Dean said. He was trying to get Kurt off of him, but to no avail.

"You know, once all of this holiday shit is over, you and I need to find some time alone," Kurt said.

"I thought you guys only played together."

"Some rules were made to be broken. God, you're handsome."

The doorbell rang and Dean was finally able to push Kurt off of him.

"You've got guests. Wouldn't want to keep them out in the cold."

Kurt laughed a bit. "I might need to go stand in the snow just to get my dick to go down. Think about what I said."

Dean went to the kitchen to find his friends, stopping a few times along the way to say hello to various people that he knew. Despite the feelings of isolation he had been experiencing lately, he knew that this extended family of his was a great group of people. They could drift in and out of each other's lives, but when they reconnected, it was almost as if no time had passed. After his nomadic upbringing, he appreciated the familiarity and comfort that he felt when they were all together.

He reached the kitchen and found Moose holding out a drink to him. The drink came with a 'disapproving look' chaser, but he took the drink anyway.

"We thought we'd lost you," Tony said. He didn't know much about Dean, but he was savvy enough to know what had just happened.

"Sorry about that," Dean said. He could feel the heat rising in his cheeks yet again.

"Does he always blush so much?" Tony asked Peter.

"Only if he really likes someone," Peter responded, enjoying the torment that Dean was feeling.

Dean gulped his drink and tried not to look at Tony. The

truth was that he *was* very attracted to the well built Italian in front of him. If he had to create the perfect man, Tony just might be him. At five feet, ten inches, Tony was just slightly taller than Dean, but he had a good 30 pounds of muscle on him. His dark hair was starting to turn silver at the temples and was cut very short. He was clean shaven, but you could tell that when he woke up in the morning, the man was scruffy. Setting it all off were the most beautiful dark eyes that Dean had ever seen. They barely knew each other, but whenever Tony looked at him, he felt that he was staring right into his soul.

"Okay, Dean's suffered enough. Let's go mingle," Moose said.

For the next hour, the foursome made their way through the crowd, stopping to chat with various groups of friends. Dean found that he was finally able to relax around Tony. The more time he spent with him, the more he realized how genuinely nice he seemed. Not just nice, but centered as well. It was as if he didn't have a care in the world. But at the same time, there was a deep soulfulness about him that drew Dean in.

Eventually, Dean and Tony found themselves alone. Dean plopped down on the couch, exhausted by all of the merry making. Tony sat next to him and put his hand on Dean's knee as he turned towards him to talk. It was the simplest of touches and yet, to Dean, it was magic.

"So, I've just got to ask this. What business does someone like you have being single?" Tony asked.

"Someone like me?"

"Yes, you're funny, smart, successful, and cute as hell. Why hasn't someone managed to tie you down?"

"Tie me down? Keep the kinky stuff to yourself, big guy," Dean joked. He was incredibly flattered that someone like Tony would find him attractive, but he wanted desperately to change the subject to anything other than himself.

"First, who says tying you down is kinky?" Tony asked, as he flashed Dean a wicked smile. "And second, don't change the subject. You're a doll, why aren't you married?"

"Trust me, I'm nothing special. I'm just an average guy. As for being single, well, that's a longer story. I traveled for work for a lot of years and that made things complicated. Even now, I tend to work a lot, and that also makes things complicated. But ultimately, I don't know, maybe it's just me, but it seems so hard to meet someone that I can connect with, especially as I get older."

"I can understand that. I was in a relationship for just over ten years. He passed away a couple of years ago. Since then, there haven't been that many quality men that have caught my interest. Until recently, that is."

"So where are you going for the holidays?" Dean asked, feeling the blood rush to his face once again.

"That might have been the most graceless change of subject I have ever heard," Tony said.

Dean laughed loudly, drawing looks from people around the room and a big smile from Tony.

"To answer your question, I'm heading to Boston. My family is there. I have 6 brothers and sisters and about nine thousand nieces and nephews. It's insanity every year, but we always have a great time. Are you going home to see your family or are you staying here?"

"Do you remember the guy you saw me with that night at Moose and Peter's house?" Dean asked.

"Lonny? Sure," Tony replied. He could see the look of surprise on Dean's face. "Oh, I've done my homework, Mister."

"You're too much. Anyway, I always spend the holidays with Lonny and his family. My parents are deceased."

"Ah. Well it's nice that you have your friend's family then," Tony said. He could sense a sadness in Dean related to the talk of his family and that was not how he wanted the evening to go. He was just about to change the subject when the subject was changed for him. Again, however, it was done without grace.

"Mistletoe!" Kurt exclaimed. He inserted himself between

them and planted a very passionate kiss on Dean, then got up and walked away.

"Damn drive-by mistletoe attacks," Dean muttered.

"You two seem close," Tony said. There wasn't anything judgmental in the statement, but Dean could tell it demanded an explanation.

"I'm close with all of my friends. But Kurt and Bill, that's a bit complicated."

"You mean since you slept with them?" Tony asked, again without judgment. He had to laugh as Dean's eyes grew to about twice their normal size. "Like I said, I did my homework."

"We all do things that in hindsight may not have been the smartest decisions. But sometimes...sometimes you just want to be with someone. Does that make sense? Why on earth am I telling you this?"

He couldn't believe he was opening up to someone he had just met. Either there was something really special about Tony, or he had already had too much vodka.

"Hypothetically, if you found yourself dating a moderately charming Italian lawyer, what are your views on monogamy?" Tony asked.

"I think you should be more concerned about my views on dating a lawyer. Just kidding. Look, just because I've slept with a few couples, doesn't mean that I would want to sleep with others if I was *part* of a couple."

"A few couples? Plural?" Tony asked, a bit more shocked than he thought he would be.

"Oh god, we are officially changing the subject."

"Actually, we do need to change the subject," Tony said, as he looked at his watch. "I have to leave in a few minutes. I promised my boss that I would stop by her party for a bit."

"Wow, I guess I shouldn't have brought up the thing about couples," Dean said. He was surprised by how disappointed he was that Tony was leaving.

"No, seriously, I made a commitment and commitments are

very important to me. I wish I could stay here and talk to you all night. As for the couples thing, don't sweat it. We all have our past. Lord knows I'm no saint. How about we worry about the future instead? Speaking of which, I'd like to see you again."

Tony had taken Dean's hand, trying to reassure him that it wasn't anything he had said that was forcing him to leave. Dean felt strength in Tony's hand. He felt warmth. It was, as it seemed with all things about Tony, an amazing feeling.

"I think seeing you again would be great," Dean said.

"Give me a second, and then walk me out?"

Dean waited on the couch as Tony went to get his coat. He was immediately joined by Moose.

"Well?" Moose asked.

"Well what? We were just talking. He has to go to another party."

Moose wanted to press Dean further, but Tony reappeared.

"Hey there," Tony said to Moose. "Sorry we didn't get to spend much time together, but I was slightly preoccupied."

"You're forgiven. But only if you come to our New Year's Eve party. Dean will be back from Florida by then, won't you Dean?"

"Yes, dear," Dean said. He had given up all pretenses that this wasn't the world's most obvious hook-up.

They all laughed as they were joined by Kurt and Bill, who also realized that Tony was leaving.

"Leaving so soon?" Bill asked. The disappointment was evident on his face.

"And leaving poor Dean alone? For shame! Don't worry, we'll take care of him for you," Kurt said.

"Behave," Bill said. He clearly wasn't in the mood.

"Thanks again for letting me come to your party. I really had a great time."

"It was our pleasure, really," Bill said. "I hope we get to see more of you."

"I'd like that," Tony replied. He kissed Bill on the cheek

and gave Kurt a brief hug.

"I'll be back in a minute. I'm going to walk Tony out," Dean said.

Once outside, Dean noticed how quiet it was. The snow had stopped falling and everything was still and beautiful.

"I'm not spending the night here, if that's what you're wondering," Dean said.

"I wasn't wondering, but would it be bad of me to say that I'm glad to hear it?"

Dean was about to respond when the door opened and Moose scurried out to join them. He quickly shoved something in Dean's front pocket.

"Virgin mistletoe," Moose whispered, then scampered back inside the house, giggling the whole time.

"Our friends, you have to love them," Dean said

"They're sweet. Can't let that go to waste, you know?" With that, he kissed Dean. Stars and rockets didn't even begin to describe how the kiss made Dean feel. When Tony pulled away, the both stood momentarily shocked by the impact they were having on each other.

"Wow," Dean finally managed to say.

"No kidding. Listen, you're freezing, you should get inside. I'll see you New Year's Eve? Maybe I can get another one of those kisses?"

"Just one?" Dean asked.

Tony carefully made his way down the snow covered stairs.

"It'll do for a start. Have a Merry Christmas, Dean. I had a wonderful time tonight."

"Me too," Dean said.

Tony walked away and Dean went back inside. It seemed like a long time until New Year's Eve.

CHAPTER 10

hortly after noon, two days before Christmas, Dean's plane miraculously landed on time at Jacksonville International Airport. After picking up his rental car, he drove south on I-95. Any time that he gained from his on-time arrival was quickly consumed by the drive south to Saint Augustine. Jacksonville, in its zeal to make itself into a large city, had been upgrading its roads and highways seemingly forever. By the time he reached the section of I-95 near The Avenues shopping mall, which was clogged with shoppers *and* undergoing construction, he thought he was going to go postal. Traffic eased a bit after the mall, but then as he got close to his turn off at State Road 16, it began to build again.

When he was growing up, this area was a backwater section of northern Florida. Now, with the World Golf Hall of Fame, two outlet malls and dozens of restaurants, it was turning into just as big a tourist trap as the rest of the state. Exiting onto 16, he drove half a mile, past every conceivable gas station and fast food joint and took a right on Green Acres

Road. As if growing up in a trailer park wasn't bad enough, he actually had to suffer the indignity of living on a street named Green Acres Road.

He drove the familiar path to the trailer in which he had spent much of his youth. It amazed him that it was still there. It had been old when he lived there and it was decrepit now. Two young children played in the front yard in their underwear, as if it were the most natural thing in the world.

He could still remember the first time Lonny had visited him here when they were children. Dean had been to a number of sleepovers at Lonny's house, but had never let Lonny visit the trailer. Finally, he relented. He can still remember the embarrassment he felt when Lonny and his Mother drove up on a Saturday afternoon. He could see the look of pity on her face as she surveyed the ramshackle piece of crap he lived in. He could also see a bit of nervousness in her eyes at the thought of leaving her son there overnight. They ended up having a good time, despite the difference in their backgrounds. Two weeks later, however, the county sheriff arrested three people who lived in the trailer park for drug trafficking. Needless to say, Lonny was never allowed to visit Dean again.

Dean wasn't sure why he had come here. He actually hadn't seen the place in years, and really had no desire to see it again. But just driving in front of the old place brought back a flood of memories, all of them bad. He hit the gas and headed back to the highway.

Twenty minutes later, eight miles east, two miles north, and a world away from his childhood, he pulled into the driveway of Lonny's parents – Connie and Donny Turnow. Lonny's brother and sister, Ronny and Bonnie, were scheduled to arrive the next day. He sat in the car for a moment as his thoughts darkened. This was the last Christmas he would ever spend with Lonny. Was this also the last Christmas he would come to Florida? Once Lonny was gone, what would he do? Lonny was his anchor and Dean did not relish the thought of being adrift. Before he could begin to truly wallow in his emotions, the front door opened and Connie came out to greet him. Dean stepped out of the car and into her warm, motherly embrace.

"Oh, you're a sight for sore eyes," Connie said as she hugged him tightly.

"It's great to see you, too, beautiful. Where is everyone?"

"Well, Lonny was a bit tired, so he's taking a nap. I sent Donny to the store to pick up some things for the party. C'mon inside and let's the two of us visit. I'm making some cookies."

She definitely knew the way to Dean's heart. They made their way to the kitchen, and she put him to work decorating the cooled batch of sugar cookies, while she prepared the next batch for the oven.

"How's Lonny doing?" Dean asked, as he meticulously decorated a gingerbread man.

"You know how it is. He has his good days and his bad days. The last couple of days haven't been so good, but he seemed a bit better this morning. I think he's better because he knew you were coming."

"I wouldn't have missed it for anything. I don't know if I've said it enough, but you guys having me here every Christmas means the world to me."

"Well, you know how much we love you. And let me tell you something, Dean Davenport, I want you here every year. No matter what happens. You hear me?"

"Yes, ma'am," Dean replied. The visit was already getting a bit too emotional for his tastes and he was unsure what to say next. Fortunately, at that point, Lonny ambled into the room, having just woken up from his nap.

"DeeDee! You're here," Lonny said, before hugging Dean. After they parted, Dean just looked at him.

"You need a shower," Dean said.

"Blow me," Lonny said, as he grabbed a half-decorated Santa Clause from Dean's hand and bit off his head.

"Lonny!" Connie said.

"Sorry for the language, Mother."

"To hell with the language. Stop eating the damn cookies.

They're for tomorrow."

The three of them broke out in a fit of laughter. They were, again, just family and friend having a good time at the holiday. After Donny returned, the four of them spent the rest of the day getting the house ready for Connie and Donny's annual Christmas Eve party. Dean felt the stress melt away and he allowed himself to enjoy the warmth of his adopted family. Beginning tomorrow there would be a succession of parties and dinners and events involving various members of Lonny's family in Northern Florida. But for now, it was just the four of them, and it was wonderful.

* * * * *

Hours later, after everyone else had gone to bed, Dean sat alone in the family room admiring the Christmas tree. For all of his hardness, he loved Christmas. Maybe it was because it was the end of the year, maybe because everyone seemed a little happier. When he realized that he couldn't sleep, he had gotten up and turned on the tree. Then he lit all of the candles in the room. It was beautiful. He was a bit startled when Lonny crept in and joined him.

"Did I wake you?" Dean whispered.

"Nah, I slept so much today that I'm not really that tired." He sat down next to Dean and huddled against him for warmth, even though it really wasn't that chilly in the room. Dean took the throw that was next to him and covered Lonny and himself with it.

"So what are you doing up?" Lonny asked.

"Couldn't sleep either. Just thinking."

"About?"

"My Mom, of all things. She would have loved this. You know, when I got accepted to Florida State, one of the first things I thought was that I was finally on my way to making something of myself. The first one in my family to go to college. I'd get a good job and I'd be able to give my Mom a little bit of what we had missed out on all of those years when I was growing up. When I think about what happened...it's not fair, you know?"

"I know, sweetie. You've gotten a raw deal over the years. For what it's worth, you've turned out to be a pretty amazing person. You really are something special. You know that, don't you?"

"I suppose."

"Ugh, what am I going to do with you?"

"What am I going to do *without* you, Lonny? I'm going to be all alone."

"What are you talking about? You have a lot of friends in Chicago, and you'll always have my family. You know they love you like a son. Hell, my mother will hunt you down if you aren't here at Christmas every year."

"Yes, she's already mentioned that."

"So what is this really about then?"

Dean laughed softly. "I think I might be having a midlife crisis. I'm pushing forty and what have I got to show for it? I go home every night to an empty apartment. I haven't been in love in so long that I've almost forgotten what it feels like. I have no roots. I could disappear tomorrow and I can't help but wonder if anyone would even notice."

"Self-pity isn't a pretty color on you. We've had this conversation before. You really have got to let go of the past. I know it's hard, but maybe you should think about what you have, rather than what you've lost. You have so much going for you. Just be happy."

"Oh, is that all I need to do?"

"It's easier than you think. Not to get all heavy on you, but someone in my position has a better perspective on a lot of things. Honey, life is short. You're going to die someday. Maybe sooner, maybe later, who knows? But when you look back, how do you want to remember your life. I worry about you so much some times. I'd give anything for you to be able to see yourself the way the rest of us do. I think you'd really like the Dean that we all know and love."

"I know this is difficult for you to understand, but do you know how hard it is to hope for a better life when everyone you have ever loved has been taken away from you? When you always end up losing anything that matters?

"But that doesn't mean you stop loving, Dean. It means that when you do love, you just love that much stronger."

"When did you get so deep?"

"I'm not sure. I think it might be the pain pills."

And with that, they were giggling. It was like the years had vanished and they were eleven years old again. The more they tried to stifle their laughter, the worse it got. It was a wonderful feeling and Dean pushed away thoughts about the future and what would happen when Lonny was no longer there to pick him up.

CHAPTER 11

I t was finally New Year's Eve. The end of the year. The
end of the holiday season. The end of traveling. The end
of the endless round of parties. So many people seemed to
bitch about going back to work in January, with the long winter
months of work stretching out in front of them, but for Dean it
was a time of renewal.

He had just finished getting ready for Moose and Peter's
party when his cell phone rang.

"Hey sexy, we're downstairs," Kurt said.

"I'll be right down," Dean said. Chicago had turned
miserably cold while he was in Florida and he had accepted
Kurt's offer of avoiding public transportation. He ran
downstairs and hopped in the car.

"Hello boys. Thanks again for the ride. It's fucking
freezing out there."

"Oh, you know we'll give you a ride anytime you want,
handsome," Kurt replied, with a wink to Dean in the rearview
mirror.

"Wow, three seconds before the first lewd remark. That

must be some sort of new record. I imagine next my wonderful hubby will tell you that he'd also be happy to ride you all the way home," Bill said.

"We *are* driving him home, to our house," Kurt said. They exchanged a cold look that told Dean this discussion had been going on for awhile. It occurred to him that the frigidness of the evening wasn't going to be limited to the city streets.

They drove the rest of the way in relative silence, with Kurt trying to make small talk, while Bill sat in stony silence and Dean made the occasional noncommittal response.

"I understand Tony is going to be at the party tonight," Bill said finally, as Kurt slowly drove around the snow covered blocks, desperately looking for parking. "So, Dean, what's going on with you two? I understand sparks were flying at our house before Christmas."

"He seems like a nice guy. Moose and Peter like him quite a bit," Dean said, trying to find a response that would cause the least amount of trouble.

"Whatever. Don't let him fool you. He's got quite the temper under that smooth exterior," Kurt said.

"Gee, what must that be like?" Bill observed dryly.

Dean knew when to keep his mouth shut. There was obviously something going on between Kurt and Bill and he did not want to get in the middle of it. The problem was, of course, that Dean being in the middle *was* the problem.

He sat quietly and studied the two lovers in the front seat. It was amazing how different they were compared to Moose and Peter. Both couples had been together for roughly the same amount of time. Both couples were made up of one partner who was more of an extrovert and one who was more of an introvert. And both couples, on occasion, brought someone else into their bed. But the essence of their relationships was completely different. Sure, Moose and Peter had the occasional argument, who didn't? But their marriage seemed so much more fulfilling than Kurt and Bill's. Moose and Peter seemed to genuinely enjoy being around each other. But Kurt and Bill were different. There seemed to be an undercurrent of darkness between them. They hadn't always been this way. But during the last year or so, certainly long before they had slept with Dean, he had noticed that things just seemed wrong between them.

When they finally arrived, the party was in full swing. Dean took Kurt and Bill's coats to the guest bedroom so that he could get away from them. The tension had not eased up during the remainder of the parking excursion and he had had enough of it. He sat down on the bed next to the pile of coats and tried to steady himself before heading back to the party. He was just about ready to walk back out when Moose entered, carrying another pile of coats.

"What are you doing in here?" Moose asked, throwing the coats on the ever growing and ever more precariously balanced pile.

"Avoiding drama. Or as I like to call it, 'The Kurt and Bill Show.'"

"Does any of this drama involve you?"

"Don't go there, Moose, seriously. I don't need a lecture right now."

"No, but you look like you could use a drink. *A small drink*. And I think there might be someone near the bar who will be very happy to see you."

"You're nothing, if not tenacious," Dean said.

They went into the living room and Moose guided them toward the bar where Peter and Tony were carrying on a conversation with Erik and Terrell. Thankfully, Kurt and Bill seemed to have wandered off somewhere else. Tony's eyes lit up as they approached and Dean cursed himself as he felt himself blushing once again. After taking the drink that Moose had made for him, Dean moved into the group next to Tony who slipped his arm around Dean and tucked his hand into his left back pocket to pull him close.

"How was your holiday?" Dean asked.

"It was great. My baby sister is pregnant again. I swear to

God, they are out of control," Tony said.

"Those damn straight people. All they think about is sex," Erik deadpanned.

"How was your Christmas, Dean? How's Lonny doing?" Terrell asked.

"It was good. He was good. We had a wonderful time. He sends his love to everyone."

The conversation moved on to other topics and they all joked and laughed during the hours leading up to midnight. Tony remained close to Dean's side. They managed to keep away from Kurt and Bill for the most part. It was a nice feeling, just being with Tony, Dean realized. He felt very comfortable with Tony's arm wrapped around him.

As it grew close to midnight, everyone started passing around hats and noisemakers. For just a moment, he wished Lonny was with them, but he let it pass and took the champagne glass that Tony was handing him. Everyone gathered in the living room as the television began counting down the last minutes to the beginning of the New Year.

Dean should have known that things were running too smoothly. Kurt and Bill approached Tony and Dean, who were standing with Erik and Terrell. Moose and Peter joined them all, to be near their friends.

"Here, something for you to blow at midnight," Kurt said, extending a noisemaker to Dean. "But don't worry, I have something else for you to blow later."

There was a ripple of nervous laughter through the group. Bill, quite noticeably, didn't laugh at all. In fact, if anyone had looked closely, they would have seen an odd expression on his face, a mix of anger and resignation. Kurt pulled Bill along as he pushed his way into the small circle next to Dean.

"I need to be near both of my guys at midnight," Kurt said.

Tony took two glasses of champagne off a tray that was being passed around and handed them to Kurt and Bill. He then deftly reinserted himself into the circle, this time positioning himself between Kurt and Dean.

"All right everyone, it's almost midnight!" Moose yelled to the crowd.

The countdown began and built to a raucous crescendo. When midnight finally arrived, Tony wrapped Dean in his arms and gave him another of his patented, amazing kisses. They were surrounded by dozens of drunk, loud, wonderful, gay men, but they might as well have been the only two people in the world.

"Here's to a great new year," Tony whispered into Dean's ear. Then he kissed him again.

The moment ended too soon and then the crowd was back and everyone was hugging and kissing and wishing each other a happy New Year. Dean noticed out of the corner of his eye that Kurt was making his way toward them. Kurt planted a quick peck on Tony's cheek before turning to give Dean a kiss that was clearly going to be much more passionate. Dean, however, had had enough for one night. He turned at the last minute and Kurt ended up mashing into the side of his head. He was not amused, and was about to let Dean know it, when Peter slipped between them for his hugs and kisses.

"Thank you," Dean whispered.

"I am nothing if not a good host," Peter replied, before moving on.

An hour later, after watching Dean yawn one too many times, Tony offered to take him home. Dean tried to protest that he was fine and that Tony didn't need to go out of his way, but his argument lost credibility when he yawned again in the middle of it. After digging through the pile of coats, every one of which seemed to be a black leather jacket, they each donned their black leather jacket and went off to find Moose and Peter, who were unfortunately talking to Kurt and Bill.

"Are you two leaving?" Moose asked. He was happily plastered but still coherent enough to be thrilled that things seemed to be going so well between Dean and Tony.

"Yeah, I'm wiped," Dean said. "Tony's going to give me a lift home."

"Just a lift," Tony said, in response to the simultaneous eyebrow arching from the group.

"I thought we were going to give you a ride home?" Kurt asked, coldly.

"Dean obviously prefers a different ride," Bill said.

"Now, ladies, let's not start the New Year off with nastiness," Moose said.

After the fastest round of kisses and goodbyes possible, they were out the door and in Tony's Mercedes.

"So that was a bit tense," Tony said.

"That's certainly one way to put it. I think I'm going to avoid those two for awhile."

"Can't say as I blame you. Can I ask you something?"

"Sure."

"If I hadn't offered to drive you home, would you have spent the night with them?"

"No, although Kurt had apparently decided for all of us that I was going to," Dean said, before relating the conversation that had occurred on the drive to the party. "Even if you weren't in the picture, I was done with that. There is something heavy going on between those two and I don't want to be in the middle of it. The last thing I want is to cause them trouble or lose their friendship."

"I'm in the picture, am I?"

"Oh, you are definitely in the picture." Dean said. He sighed and settled into the leather seats as the car quickly warmed up.

"That was a happy sigh."

"I feel relaxed. It's a rare feeling for me. I'm very comfortable around you."

"Would you like to be comfortable around me Thursday night at a nice restaurant of your choosing?"

"Hmmm, I might have to get back to you on that. I need to dig out my 'How to Date a Man' handbook and figure out the proper protocols on timing, place, attire – it's been a long time."

"How about we forget the rulebooks and just enjoy getting to know each other?" Tony asked, as he took Dean's hand.

"Thursday it is, then," Dean said, punctuating it with another contented sigh.

CHAPTER 12

The week after New Year's Day was unusually slow at the foundation. On Wednesday, with most of his staff still on their vacations, Dean allowed himself the luxury of a very long lunch with Moose - and maybe some post holiday shopping. Just as he left the building, his cell phone rang. He recognized the area code as Lonny's, but not the phone number.

"Hello?"

"Hey you," Lonny said. There was a weakness in his voice that chilled Dean.

"Where are you?" Dean asked.

"First, let me say that I'm okay."

"Lonny, what's going on?" Dean asked. He had stopped in the middle of the sidewalk, forcing the crowd of shoppers to go around him.

"It's nothing, really. I fainted last night, so they brought me to the hospital for observation. They're going to let me go home in a few hours."

"Why didn't you call me?"

"Well, DeeDee, I was slightly unconscious at the time."

"You know what I mean."

"I'm okay. I just haven't been eating enough and my blood counts were all out of whack. I've been duly lectured by all of the appropriate doctors and parental units and it won't happen again."

"Should I come back down?" He was fully prepared to hop on the next plane to Florida.

"Don't be insane. I just fainted. I'm fine. Anyway, what are you doing?"

Dean took a breath before answering. It had always been his fear that he would receive a call like this, from a number that he didn't recognize and that someone on the other end would tell him that Lonny was gone. The reality of Lonny's situation hit him again like a ton of bricks, and for just a moment he thought he was going to break down right there in the middle of the street. He took another deep breath and pulled himself together. The call would come someday, but it wasn't today, and there was no need to upset Lonny.

"Um, hello? Earth to DeeDee."

"Sorry, I got distracted. What were you saying?" Dean asked.

"Aw, sweetie, did you see something shiny in one of the windows? I know how that can throw you off your stride. I asked you what you are doing."

"I'm meeting Moose for lunch at Field's, little Miss Hateful."

"You know, when I spoke with Moose on New Year's Day, he mentioned that you and this Tony person seemed to be hitting it off quite well. In fact, Moose tells me that you have a date with Tony tomorrow night. I bring this up because, as I mentioned, Moose told me. Somehow, this news didn't seem to make it into any of the conversations that I have had with you since New Year's Eve."

"I didn't want to make a big deal out of it. He seems like a nice guy and we're going out on a date. It's nothing major."

"I would hardly call you going on a date *nothing major*. It's like a lunar eclipse. Sure, it happens every now and then, and sure, everyone knows what it looks like, but it happens so infrequently that it still makes the news. Also, according to the emails that I've been getting from Peter, this guy is something special. I hear that you are blushing non-stop when you're around him."

"It's nice to see that we've graduated to cross-country gossip. Technology is such a marvelous thing. I'm sure this is exactly what the creators of the internet had in mind when they first came up with the idea."

"What's going on? They tell me you light up around this guy, and now you're saying it's no big deal?"

"I just don't want to get my hopes up. I've dated a lot of great guys over the years and for some reason it never works out. I'm tired of the disappointment. If something happens, great. If not, I'm not going to stress out over it."

"Would this be an appropriate time to point out that the only common factor in all of your failed dating experiments is you?" Lonny asked, sweetly.

"I'm glad you're feeling better, now I don't feel so bad about calling you a bitch."

"All kidding aside, Dean, do you remember when we first moved to Chicago? You were like a kid in a candy store. I mean, sure, you were slutty, but you were also excited about dating back then. What happened?"

"We aren't going to have this conversation while I'm walking down the street. I'm going on the date and we'll see what happens," Dean said, irritated by the pressure that Lonny was putting on him. "Look, I'm at Fields, so I need to hang up. If anything happens with your health, you call me. Do you understand?"

"Yes, dear. But I want to hear everything about the date on Friday morning."

Dean hung up and made his way through the store to the men's clothing section where he found Moose perusing the sale rack of ties.

"Anything interesting?" Dean asked. Moose was completely absorbed by the array of ties in front of him.

"Oh good, you're wearing a blue shirt. Take off your coat."

"Typical man. No hello, no how are you, just take off your clothes," Dean said. He shrugged off his coat and watched as Moose started throwing ties over his shoulders. Moose was a shopping phenom. Within ninety seconds he had compared and contrasted a dozen different ties and settled on buying four.

"You're a freak," Dean said.

"I'm efficient. Let's go eat, I'm starving."

"Okay, but when we're done, remind me to hang you with one of those ties you just bought."

"Why? What'd I do?" Moose asked.

"Why are you gabbing to Lonny so much about my date with Tony? He's giving me grief because I didn't tell him."

"Sweetie, its all anyone is talking about."

"God, Chicago in winter is so boring. Just try not to talk it up so much to Lonny. He thinks I'm on the verge of marrying this guy."

They made their way to the escalator bank for the trip to the seventh floor. By the time their criss-crossing journey had taken them to the fifth floor, Moose had counted no less than four guys who had cruised Dean.

"I hate going out with you. No one ever looks at me. Everyone always wants the cute little guy."

"First, I am not a little guy. You just happen to be abnormally large. I mean tall, yes, that's it, tall. Second, the sum total of yours and Peter's extracurricular activities last year hardly lends credence to the argument that no one ever looks at you."

"That's true. You always know just what to say to make me feel better." Moose started playfully poking Dean in the chest. "Are you excited about the date? Are you? Are you?"

"Stop poking me you giant freak. I swear sometimes you don't know how much that hurts. Now, if the date goes well, I won't be able to get naked because he'll see all the bruises on my chest and think I'm some sort of pain fetishist."

"Aren't you? Wait a minute...don't change the subject."

"I'm sorry, what was the subject?"

"Are you excited about the date?"

"Christ, why is everyone putting so much pressure on me about this date? Yes, I'm excited. Yes, he's a nice guy. Yes, I'm looking forward to the date. Should I set up a web page with hourly announcements counting down to the big event? That way you guys can all stop hounding me?"

"Why are you getting so cranky?" Moose asked. He then poked Dean again, for no other reason than he was there.

"*Ow!* Stop it! I'm cranky because everyone seems to think that this is the last date that I'm ever going to have. It's just a fucking date. You know, it *is* entirely possible that we won't hit it off."

"That is *so* not going to happen. We all see the way you guys look at each other. We haven't seen you like this in a long time. It's so cute!"

"Well, I wouldn't say all of you. Kurt called me yesterday. He was warning me again that Tony has his not-so-charming moments. He said that when Tony and Steve were together they fell off the face of the earth because Tony was always so jealous of everyone. And, if you think about it, he has a point because I don't ever remember meeting Tony and we're all a pretty tight group."

"Kurt needs to shut the fuck up. He doesn't want you dating anyone because he wants you for himself, which is just selfish and, frankly, weird. As for Tony and Steve, you never met them because they were always more Peter's friends than part of the group. And yes, they did tend to keep to themselves, but they were always quite nice when we were around them. I swear, I'm going to kill Kurt. I don't know why he wants to ruin this for you guys."

"See, that's what I'm talking about. There is no 'this' to be ruined. We haven't even had one date yet. You and Lonny are picking out china patterns for me already. Seriously, you guys are freaking me out more than Kurt possibly could."

"I'm sorry, honey, I just want you to be happy."

"And a single person can't be happy?"

"You know what? I apologize. You're right. You can be perfectly happy on your own. I'm sorry that I'm putting so much pressure on you. You know I love you."

"I know, honey. Let's just have lunch and not talk about it anymore. Okay?"

"Deal."

Still, in the back of his mind, despite all of his words to the contrary, he knew that Moose was right about one thing - Tony was indeed special. And even though he was downplaying the date, he was surprised to find that he really was looking forward to finding out just how special Tony might be.

CHAPTER 13

Dean sat at the bar of the Gold Coast steak house that he and Tony had settled on for their date, he anxiously checked his watch for the tenth time in the last five minutes. Tony was fifteen minutes late and Dean's nerves were getting more wrecked by the minute. He knew there was no way that he was going to be stood up, but that didn't matter. It was a first date and every insecurity he had ever felt was bubbling up to the surface. The biggest one, of course, was the realization that Tony was too good for him and that somehow he had finally figured this out and was on a plane bound for Bangladesh, never to be seen again.

Get a grip, he thought, you're being stupid. He wasn't being stood up. He should stop obsessing. Why *was* he obsessing? Was it because it was a first date? Was it because it he hadn't been on any sort of date, first, second or tenth, in months? Was it because it he liked Tony so much? When it dawned on him that he had reached the point where he was obsessing about why he was obsessing, he decided that he really needed another drink.

The bartender was just setting his martini down when Tony rushed into the restaurant, looked around a bit more frantically than he probably wanted to, and then hurried over to the bar and kissed Dean on the cheek.

"I am so sorry," Tony said, He grabbed a napkin and wiped the sweat off his forehead. "I'm never late, I swear. I can't believe I'm late."

Dean couldn't help but laugh. "It's ten degrees outside, how can you be sweating?"

"I ran six blocks to get here. I mean *ran*. This nightmare of a case I'm working on blew up around four o'clock. I was on a conference call trying to fix everything while everyone was blaming everyone else for the clusterfuck that has happened. I kept looking at my watch, knowing that I was going to be late. I wanted to call you, but I couldn't get off the phone. Then I find out I have to go to San Francisco tomorrow for a day trip. A day trip! It has not been a good day."

Dean tried not to laugh any more, but he couldn't help it. Every time he had been with Tony he seemed so smooth and together, like not a thing in the world could faze him. There was something endearing about the flushed, sweaty mess in front of him that made Dean realize that maybe they should both relax a bit and try to enjoy themselves.

"Take a breath, and a drink, and relax. You're here and we have all night."

The maitre'd came over and escorted them to their table. It was a secluded booth in the back and, for that, Dean was grateful. Despite his best efforts to overcome his conservative upbringing, there were still times when he was uncomfortable going on a date at a primarily straight venue. It helped that the server who came over to see if they needed another drink was a cute young woman who obviously realized they were on a date and clearly couldn't care less. She immediately put them both at ease and they worked through their orders.

"So what type of law do you practice?" Dean asked, after the server went to get their appetizers and a bottle of wine.

"Intellectual property rights as they relate to the creation of medical devices," Tony said, as if it were just an everyday thing.

"Okay, my head hurts just from hearing you say it. I can't imagine what it must be like dealing with it every day."

Tony laughed. "Normally, it's great. The people I deal with are fascinating and the law is exciting. Today, however, it sucked ass. So let's change the subject. What do you do?"

"I'm Chief Operating Officer at a research foundation."

"Wow! Smell you!"

"Well, it's not as impressive as it sounds. I mean, it's not like I'm the COO of some multi-national corporation. We're pretty large as far as foundations go, but small compared to a lot of businesses."

"Do you like it?"

"I do, actually. I'm not a doctor or anything like that, but I've always felt that doing what I do allows me to help the doctors a little bit as they go about trying to cure diseases and help people. It lets me feel like I'm contributing something instead of just doing a job."

"So, you're noble and cute. Nice combination," Tony said, with a wink.

"Ah, I'm not so special. Anyway, enough about work. So, how is it possible that you and I have never met? It's a small gay world, especially when you run in the same circle of friends."

"See how you are? We have met. It was about six years ago."

"No way, I would have remembered."

"Probably not. I was with Steve then and we didn't go out much. But we were close with Peter and Moose. Steve and Peter met in college. Over the years we drifted apart a bit, but every now and then we would make our way to one of their infamous parties. I think it was either an IML party or someone's birthday, but I distinctly remember you. Don't get me wrong, I'm a firm believer in monogamy – shocking, I know – but when I see someone like you, I notice. I'm only human."

Much to his chagrin, Dean felt his face turn red again. "I swear there will come a time when I don't blush every time I'm around you."

"I think it's adorable."

"Fine, then you start doing it. So why were you and Steve such recluses?"

"Well, it wasn't like we planned it or anything. I honestly don't know how Moose and Peter do it. They have their jobs and their relationship and this amazing social life with all of their friends. When Steve and I were together, there never seemed to be enough time to do anything. When the weekends came around, we were so busy with the house and so busy just being together that everything else seemed to fall by the wayside. Then, during the last couple of years, when he was sick, it was pretty much just the two of us and I lost touch with everyone, except Peter and Moose. In a way, what's going on now is kind of sweet. I get to rediscover my friends."

Dean had an odd look on his face. "You know, I remember them talking about their friend Steve who was sick. I was on the road at the time so we never talked about it that much. If I recall correctly, they said you two had a great relationship."

"We did. After he passed away, it took awhile for me to realize that I might be able to meet someone again. It's only lately that I've started going on dates again. Just a few dates here and there, but nothing major. Well, until recently."

"Oh? Anyone I know?"

"Intimately. Anyway, a couple of months ago, I ran into Peter in the Loop. We started having lunch every now and then, which is how I ended up at their Christmas party a few weeks ago. Lucky for me."

"Lucky for both of us," Dean said, as he raised his glass in a small toast.

"Speaking of that night, how is your friend Lonny doing?"

"He's as well as can be expected. I don't know how much

Peter might have told you, but Lonny's dying. It's hard, as I'm sure you can imagine. I suppose it doesn't matter if it's a friend or a lover or family member, when you love somebody that much, the thought of losing them is sometimes too much to deal with. I'm trying to just focus on him and being there for him. I'm trying not to think about the part that comes after."

"Believe it or not, you'll survive. And you'll be thankful that you had the time with him that you're having now."

"Okay, this may not be the best discussion we could be having on a first date. Let's change the subject again," Dean suggested.

"Fair enough. But for what it's worth, you're amazingly easy to talk to, regardless of the subject. I like that."

"Me too. That always seems to be the hardest thing about meeting someone – finding a way to communicate. It seems like so many people just have nothing to say. Or, maybe it's like you said and it's just a matter of finding a comfort level with someone."

The waitress came back with their wine. While she went through the usual show, Dean tried not to stare at Tony. Their conversation was going so well, and Tony seemed so nice, that he had almost forgotten how attractive Tony was.

"So, you asked me how I knew Peter and Moose. How about you? Or do you know them in the same way you know Kurt and Bill?" Tony asked, after the waitress departed.

"I suppose I had that coming after the comment I made about couples the last time I saw you. No, I don't know them in the biblical sense. Believe it or not, I haven't slept with every couple I know." Dean said.

"I hope you don't think I'm judging you because of what I said. It really was just a joke. Admittedly, the Italian in me would be happier if you were a virgin, but I guess that is a shortcoming I can overlook."

"Well thank God, because that is one bell that definitely cannot be unrung. Anyway, Moose and Peter. How did we meet? God, it seems like a hundred years ago. We all happened to be out at Sidetrack. Lonny and I were standing near them. I was flirting shamelessly with Moose, until I realized he was with Peter. But then they started talking to us and just like that, we were all friends. We have been ever since. They really are the sweetest guys I know. Moose is like the big brother I never had. Which, of course, also means he's a giant pain in the ass sometimes. But I do love them."

"That's sweet. And seriously, I really was kidding earlier. I don't care about your past, or mine for that matter. I'm much more concerned about how someone acts when they are with me. Not to say that you're *with me* or anything. I just mean that, you know, in the future, if we were together...oh fuck it. I surrender."

"So, basically, you're a one many guy?" Dean asked. Again, he was blown away by how charming Tony was.

"Yes, I guess that is a more succinct way of putting it. Which isn't to say to that I expect the same from you. We just met. I don't want you to think I'm asking you to marry me or anything on our first date."

"Relax. I didn't think that. You can also stop worrying about other guys. Although, I have to say, I think I'm getting laid in your head a lot more than I am in real life. Yes, I like to have my fun every now and then, but when I'm dating someone – which is rare, by the way – I just can't date more than one person, or sleep with someone else when I'm dating someone. God bless the people who can compartmentalize like that, but I've never been able to do it. Must be that repressive Southern Baptist upbringing."

"The Roman Catholic in me completely understands."

In retrospect, it was an odd conversation to have on a first date. But at the same time, Dean realized that it allowed them to reach an understanding. They were two men, each of whom had their pasts, and each of whom was dealing with different things in the present. But they also understood each other, and that would hopefully make getting to know each other a bit easier.

By the time Dean next looked at his watch, it was close to eleven. He noticed that they were one of the few tables left in the restaurant. The time had flown and he had loved every minute of it.

"So what are you doing Saturday night?" Tony asked, beating Dean to the punch by mere seconds. For once, Dean didn't blush. His smile, however, melted Tony's heart.

CHAPTER 14

Still enjoying the slow work week, Dean slept in and went into the office late the next morning. Of course, late for him was eight o'clock. When he arrived at work he had a voicemail waiting for him from Moose that told him to put down his briefcase, put his coat back on, and head around the corner to Starbuck's where he and Bill were waiting to dish about the date. Having been away from the dating game so long, he had forgotten how quickly news traveled along the gay grapevine. By the time he arrived, his friends had already had a lengthy discussion via cell phone with Peter and were midway through a detailed analysis of the big date.

Dean walked in and saw his friends sitting on a large, comfortable couch in the corner. They saw him, waved, and then began giggling like two schoolgirls. Dean rolled his eyes, and decided that he would need an extra shot of espresso in his morning cup of coffee. After picking up his drink and a muffin, he made his way over to the couch and sat down on the oversized chair next to it. Moose and Bill stopped whispering and looked at him.

"Get it over with," Dean said.

"How was the date?"

"What did you wear?"

"What did he wear?"

"Where did you go?"

"Did you make out?"

"Was there tongue involved?"

"Did you do it?"

"Did you make out, but not do it, but still manage to cop a feel of his Italian sausage?"

Dean actually spit out a little bit of muffin on the last question, thereby interrupting the very disturbing stream of consciousness they had going.

"We had a very nice time," Dean said, ensuring the maximum irritation from both of them.

"Oh, hell no," Moose said. "Don't even think you're going to get away with that."

"What? We *did* have a nice time. The food was great, the company was wonderful. It was very nice."

Moose however, wasn't an amateur when it came to playing this game. "You know what, sweetie? You're absolutely right. Who are we to pry? So, Bill, as I was saying, Peter had a very lengthy conversation this morning with Tony about the date. He said some *very* interesting things. Call me later today and we'll discuss it."

Now it was Dean's turn to squirm. "I truly, truly, hate you. I hope you realize that."

"Of course I do, that's what makes our friendship so grand!"

"What did he say?" Dean asked.

"Oh, I'm sorry, are you talking to me? I thought we weren't discussing this issue. Heaven forbid we get you to open up a bit and talk about something."

"As much as I need and cherish my morning coffee, I have utterly no qualms about throwing it on you and watching you melt away in a puff of smoke," Dean said.

"Well, since he told Peter it was one of the top three dates of his life, I think it is safe to assume that he had a pretty good time."

"Wow, he must not date very much," Dean said, his blasé attitude doing a poor job of hiding how thrilled he was to hear that Tony had enjoyed their time together as much as he had.

Bill had had enough. "Honestly, it's like pulling teeth. Tell us about the fucking date."

"It was awesome. You know how you meet someone and everything seems to click? The conversation flows, and you're attracted to him and he's attracted to you, and everything is damn near perfect? It was like that – only a little bit better."

"Yay! I'm so happy!" Moose exclaimed. "Now was that so hard?"

"I just don't want to get all worked up about it. You guys know how successful I've been when it comes to dating. I don't want to get carried away."

"Sweetie, you're allowed to feel actual emotions. We humans do it all the time and it's just a hoot!" Moose said.

"You know, Dean, I'm thrilled for you. But Kurt isn't going to like this one bit. He might be forced to sleep with just me for awhile," Bill said.

"What is that about anyway?" Moose asked.

"Who knows? Maybe he just likes Dean more than his old tried and true husband."

The conversation was suddenly making Dean very uncomfortable, especially in light of Kurt's offer that he and Dean find some time alone. He knew Bill was angry about the way their relationship was heading, but it wasn't until now that he realized how hurt he was.

"Look, Bill, I'm sorry if sleeping with you guys was a mistake. I really thought it was something that we all wanted to do. If I caused any problems..."

"Don't worry about it. I'm a big boy and I can make my own decisions. Sometimes when you're part of a couple there are compromises that you have to make. I think, on this front at least, I'm getting tired of making compromises."

"Good for you," Moose said. "You need to rein him in a bit. He's a menace to men everywhere."

"But enough about that," Bill said. "When are you two seeing each other again, Dean?"

"He's making dinner for me tomorrow night."

"Oh my god! You're totally going to do it!" Moose said.

Just the sight of the six foot five Moose exclaiming his joy at Dean's upcoming sexual good fortune was enough to get the three of them roaring with laughter, which drew stares and glares from all of the patrons in the coffee shop.

* * * * *

Later that evening, as Dean was getting ready for bed, he thought back to his conversation with Moose and Bill. Why was it so hard for him to loosen up? What exactly did he think was going to happen? He'd met a great guy who he liked and who liked him. Why couldn't he just allow himself to enjoy it? Lonny was right, when Dean had been younger he absolutely loved dating. He gave himself over to it completely. But as the years and the disappointments mounted, he started closing himself off, until finally, dating had started to seem like a chore, rather than something to be celebrated.

Dean was just about to crawl into bed when the phone rang. When he saw that it was Tony, his heart skipped a bit. Maybe the magic wasn't completely dead after all, he thought.

"Hello, handsome, did you make it home alive?" Dean said.

"Yeah. I have never been so tired in my life. I do *not* recommend day trips to the West Coast."

"Did everything get worked out?"

"Yes, I was suitably tired and cranky when I got there, so I wasn't in the mood for anyone's crap. I sat them down and we hammered things out. The good news is that my flights were on time both ways. What are you doing?"

"Just getting into bed."

"Woof. What are you wearing?"

"Wearing? I'm in bed. Who wears anything to bed?" Dean said coyly.

"Oh god, you're killing me."

"Does that mean the date is still on for tomorrow? I'll totally understand if you're exhausted and want to postpone."

"Don't even try. You *will* be here at seven o'clock tomorrow evening."

"Yes, Sir! Should I bring anything?"

"Just yourself. And maybe a toothbrush?" Tony asked.

"Ah, I see. So the Italian in you was hoping I was a virgin. Which part of you is hoping I'm going to spend the night?"

"Believe me, there are few parts of me that are hoping you're going to spend the night. Oh, you meant which part of my ethnic background? Yeah, that's the Italian part too."

"Well, I can't make any promises, but like a good scout, I'll certainly come prepared. But you never know, by the end of the night you might be tired of me."

"That seems incredibly unlikely. As a matter of fact, I may already like you too much. You seem like a really special guy."

"I'm really not."

"You know, we're going to have to teach you how to say 'thank you' when someone gives you a compliment."

"It's always been a failing of mine. One of many."

"You're impossible? You're great – and don't contradict me," Tony said, before yawning.

"You sound tired. You should get some sleep."

"That might be a good idea. Need to look my best tomorrow, after all."

"I doubt you could look bad if you tried."

"Thank you. See how easy that was? Okay, handsome man, I'm going to hit the sack. I'll see you tomorrow."

"I can't wait." Dean said, and he meant it.

They said their goodnights and Dean turned off the light.

Ten minutes earlier he had been exhausted, but now his mind raced with thoughts of Tony. He really had forgotten how wonderful this could feel - the excitement of getting to know someone, the desire to be with them both sexually and emotionally. He was surprised by how much he had missed it. He was just about to nod off when it occurred to him that at this time the following night, he'd probably be in bed with Tony. That thought kept him up for a little while longer, but in a very happy way.

CHAPTER 15

A few minutes before seven the following evening, Dean found himself in front of Tony's house. It was situated on a beautiful street of very expensive homes just south of the Lincoln Park Campus of DePaul University. For a moment, he just stood and stared. This is not doing wonders for my self-esteem, he thought. Was everything about this guy perfect? The two-story brick home in front of him was stunning. From the woodwork of the front stairs to the stained glass window in the second floor stairwell, it was a gay man's dream home.

He rang the bell and waited with anticipation. He was surprised once again by how nervous he felt. Dean assumed that after their first date, his nerves would have settled down, but he still felt like the president of the chess club about to have a date with the prom queen. Of course, a first date was one thing. This date was at Tony's home, and despite Dean's coyness, he had indeed brought along a toothbrush.

Finally, Tony opened the door and beamed at Dean then shuffled him inside.

"I hope you didn't have too much trouble finding the place," he asked as he took Dean's coat.

"Nah, no problems. You have to love Chicago's grid system, everything is easy to find," Dean said. "I picked up some wine. I've had it before. It's pretty good."

"I told you that you didn't have to bring anything."

"A gay man show up at someone's house without bringing something? Are you insane?" Dean asked, in mock horror.

Tony just laughed. "Come on into the kitchen, I've got stuff on the stove. I'll give you the tour later."

One of the things that everyone knew about Dean, and was much appreciated by all of his friends, was that he was an amazing cook. He had developed an interest in cooking from his mother. They had spent hours in the kitchen trying to make gourmet meals out of whatever food items they had found on sale that week. More often than not, they succeeded in creating something that was much greater than the sum of its parts. Because of this love of the culinary arts, Dean was stopped dead in his tracks when he walked into Tony's kitchen. It was chef heaven. Every state of the art appliance that you could ask for, marble counter tops, top-of-the-line sinks and faucets. Dean was almost speechless.

"Oh. My. God." It was all Dean was able to eke out.

"What?" Tony asked, thinking Dean had seen something repulsive. Then he made the connection. "Oh, that's right. Peter said that you were a pretty good cook. This is a bit more than I need, but I was redoing the entire house anyway, so I figured I might as well do it right."

"It's...it's amazing. I could live in here!"

Tony wrapped his arms around Dean and kissed him deeply. "I like the idea of you here cooking. That would be nice."

"When did you finish the renovations? Yesterday? Everything looks brand new," Dean said, finally recovering from the food-lover wet dream that he found himself in.

"You're not far off. I bought the house right after Steve

died. There were too many memories in the old place and I decided that life had to go on, so I bought this. The renovations took about eighteen months of real time and about fifteen years off of my life. It was quite a process."

"Well, you should be proud of yourself, it's absolutely beautiful."

"So when Peter told me that I should ask about your dream life, was this what he was talking about?"

"What?" Dean asked, with a confused look.

"I was chatting with Peter today – about you, of course – and he said that I should ask you to tell me the 'dream life' story. He said it was hysterical and I would find it particularly interesting."

"For the love of God," Dean groaned. "I'm never going to live this down. Look, here's what you need to keep in mind about this story: I was incredibly drunk. It was a few years ago. We had been out at the bars for hours and we were all pretty well lit. We decided to go the Melrose Diner to get some food and sober up. It had to be close to three in the morning at that point. For whatever reason, I was kvetching about how I never meet anyone. I was apparently getting rather loud. I said that all I wanted was a nice guy. With a nice house. And a fireplace. And a big kitchen. And a dog. And a car. And a job. And a cabin on a lake. And a furry chest. And a big...well, let's just say the list went on and on and I got louder and louder, until finally the manager had to come over and ask me to keep it down. My friends, being the living, breathing, spawns of Satan that they are have never let me forget that drunken tirade. They've actually managed to create quite a little show of reciting it verbatim for me when they really want to annoy me."

Tony was looking at the ceiling doing mental calculations for a few seconds before responding. "Yep. Everything but the dog."

"Excuse me?" Dean asked.

"The list. Everything you named. Except the dog. But I can

buy a dog," he said, smiling.

"So what are you saying? You're telling me you have a big...cabin somewhere?"

Tony laughed loudly. "The cabin is just medium sized. The size of everything else, well, that's in the eye of the beholder."

Dean shook his head. This man was too good to be true.

"Wait a minute, we need to back up a few paces. Peter said I was a *pretty good* cook. That's it? Pretty good? Do you have any idea what I made that man for his birthday last year? It took five hours!"

"Okay, let's get you a drink," Tony said as he gave Dean a corkscrew and put him to work on the wine. Tony went back to work on the dinner.

"So, in addition to being smart, adorable and a great kisser, now you tell me you're a chef, too? I just might have to marry you if you keep this up," Tony said.

"Oh believe me, I have my faults. Moody, distant, a history of familial inbreeding. You should probably run while you have the chance. I'm certainly not quite the catch that you are. You're pretty intimidating in a lot ways."

"Me? I'm a pussycat. The house, the money, all that stuff doesn't really matter. It's what's inside that counts. Unfortunately, most guys I meet seem to be quite lacking in that area. And again, you do the self-deprecation bit. What's up with that?"

"First rule of business, under promise and over deliver. It's the key to success."

"God, have we really reached the point where we can compare dating to a business transaction?"

"I'm only kidding. Sort of. Anyway, I really am just an average guy," Dean said, as he handed Tony a glass of wine.

"Well, from what I've seen the last couple of years, being an average guy puts you in the top ten percent of most of the guys out there."

"Top ten percent?" Dean asked, feigning indignation. "Last I heard, I was one of your top three dates of all time."

"Damn gossipy queens," Tony muttered, finding that it was he who was blushing for once.

"If it's any consolation, you ranked pretty high on my list, too."

"Pretty high top fifty or pretty high number one?"

"Don't fish for compliments, its undignified."

Tony laughed again and started pulling food out of the cupboards. "Can I ask you something?"

"Of course."

"Why haven't you asked me if I'm HIV positive yet? Most guys, when they find out that Steve died of AIDS, ask within five minutes of meeting me."

"I hadn't really thought about it," Dean said, truthfully. "I mean, like anyone our age, I've dated guys who are negative and guys who are positive. I can honestly say I've never treated either one differently. It's not like it really matters in the beginning. It's not as if we would have sex differently depending on what you said. I care about someone being HIV positive in the same way I would care if they had diabetes. I'd want them to take care of themselves and hope for the best."

"Not everyone feels that way."

"Well, think about it. Someone like me, who has been single most of his life and has had more than his fair share of sex, has just as good a chance, if not better, of being positive than someone who was married to someone who had AIDS."

"For what it's worth, I'm negative."

"Me too. And for what it's worth, it really wouldn't have mattered either way."

"I know this is going to be hard for you to hear but you are a very good man, Dean Davenport. I know it's a compliment, which is like kryptonite to you, but I have faith in your ability to accept it."

Dean was, in fact, about to protest, but Tony was so close, and so damn handsome, that he just kissed him instead.

CHAPTER 16

For Dean, there was always a fleeting moment before he became fully awake when it was almost impossible to tell if he was dreaming or not. That's how it was for him the next morning when he slowly drifted up from a deep, restful sleep. His head was nestled on Tony's furry chest and their bodies were comfortably entwined. He had never felt so at ease with someone in his life. When he finally did wake up, he made sure not to move, so as not to disturb Tony. Also, he didn't want to break the wonderful feeling of just lying next to such an amazing man.

Thoughts of the night before began creeping into his head and a smile drifted over his lips. The dinner had been great. Cuddling on the couch listening to some funky remixed jazz had been nice. But when they went to bed, well, that took things to an entirely different level.

Over the course of his life – the sexual part of his life, anyway – he had learned there were really only two types of men: nice guys and pigs. He usually ended up in bed with nice guys. The sex was fun, or good, or pretty good, and almost always the same. But every now and then, whether by happenstance or a rare urge, he found himself in bed with a pig. There was no agenda other than raucous, hardcore sex. It was always wild and exciting. He never imagined dating one of those men who fulfilled his more fringe desires. In his mind, it was like the old straight adage 'there are girls you fuck, and girls you marry.'

Dean had assumed that Tony would be one of the nice guys. He was, after all, a *nice guy*. He was funny and charming and considerate. There was nothing that he had seen that would lead him to believe that he would be anything different when the lights went out. But from the moment they had entered the bedroom, he had changed. He was still nice, and he was still considerate, but there was also an air of steely determination about him. The look in his eyes was different than Dean had ever seen before and he knew, without even having to ask, that this wasn't going to be an evening of polite sex. Tony had a hungry look in his eyes. The kind of look that let you know he was going to get what he wanted, come hell or high water. And over the next three hours, he did just that.

It seemed like they were barely naked before Tony was reaching into the nightstand drawer and pulling out a condom. Dean was about to give the requisite, proper protests about how 'it's only our first date' and 'go slow, its been a really long time' but before he knew what was happening, his legs were in the air and Tony's mouth was doing things to his ass that took his breath away. When Tony came up for air, Dean tried to make one more protest about propriety but within seconds, Tony's mouth was on Dean's so hard he was sure he'd leave bruises while simultaneously, he entered Dean hard, fast, and without asking permission.

The first fuck didn't take long. Tony seemed overwhelmed with lust. He bellowed Dean's name as he came, his forehead pressed against Dean's, as if he were trying to get as deep into his head as he already was in his ass. When he could finally breathe again, he kissed Dean passionately.

"God, I have wanted you from the moment I first saw you," Tony said, between ragged breaths. He reached over to the nightstand again, and Dean assumed he was getting a towel to clean them up. Instead, he pulled out another condom, and after replacing the used one, flipped Dean over and slid in again. Tony wrapped his arms, his legs and his soul around Dean's body and rode him again – hard. There was a non-stop stream of passionate and borderline filth coming from Tony's lips, which combined with the unimaginable pleasure he was giving his ass was too much for Dean. He screamed as he came, and Tony quickly followed. They each came a few more times before it was all over and then fell asleep in a heap of tangled sheets and sweat.

Lying there in the morning light, pretty much every inch of Dean's body had some sort of pleasant ache. Some spots ached more pleasantly than others, but he wouldn't have had it any other way. He wasn't sure if was the sex itself, or the way he was starting to feel about Tony, but it was by far the greatest night of pure, unadulterated passion that he had ever experienced.

"Whatcha thinking, beautiful?" Tony asked.

"Just remembering last night. That was something else."

"Yeah, sorry about that. I get carried away sometimes. I've been dying to be with you. I hope I didn't come on too strong."

"I don't think you heard too much complaining," Dean said, before yawning and stretching. "Man, I haven't felt this good in forever. I don't want to move."

"Too bad," Tony said, as he took Dean's hand and guided it down between the sheets. Tony was clearly fully awake now. And with that, they were off and running again.

* * * * *

Two hours and a shower later, they were in the kitchen having coffee. Tony read the paper while Dean finished making a couple of omelets.

"These are delicious," Tony said, moments later, between heaping mouthfuls. "What did you put in them?"

"If I told you that, you wouldn't need to invite me back."

"Oh, you're coming back. As often as you like," Tony said as he handed Dean his empty plate. "More please."

"You can't be serious."

"I think I lost a lot of protein last night, I need to rebuild my strength."

Dean went back to the stove and began working on Tony's second omelet. He couldn't remember the last time he had felt this kind of peaceful, quiet intimacy of two men alone on a Sunday morning. No pressures from work, no pressures from friends, no television, no internet, just a calm sense of serenity. The dozen errands that Dean needed to run today briefly flitted through his mind, but he willed himself to relax. The rest of the world and the demands of life could wait. He just wanted to enjoy this feeling for awhile.

"So what are your plans for the day?" Tony asked, as if he were reading Dean's mind.

"Oh, the usual. Errands, shopping, stuff like that."

"Why don't you forget all that and just hang out with me. It's Sunday for Christ's sake. The work week is for tomorrow. Let's do something fun today."

"I don't know if my backside can take much more fun," Dean said, with a wink. "Besides, if I spent the day with you, it might damage my loner reputation."

"Peter mentioned that you liked your space. He told me that I shouldn't let you get away with running off."

"Okay, for starters, you and Peter talk way too much. And second, believe it or not, I actually don't feel like running off this morning. So there."

"I'm honored."

"You should be. I guess it's true that I have a tendency to take off the first chance I get."

"Why is that?" Tony asked, as he set the paper aside to give Dean his undivided attention.

"I've never really thought about it. I guess I've been alone so long that I've just grown accustomed to it. I don't just mean alone as in single. I mean, *alone*. I don't have any brothers or sisters, my dad died when I was a kid and my mom passed away when I was in college. I've just always been on my own. Obviously I have friends and all that, but they're all couples. It just seems that more often than not, I find myself by myself. It's like anything I guess, once you get used to it, it becomes the norm."

"It's just the opposite for me. I told you I came from a large family. Then, I had all those years with Steve. I'm probably a little too uncomfortable being alone. The last couple of years in this house have certainly been an adjustment. At first, it drove me crazy. I didn't know what to do with myself. Over time, I learned how to be by myself without becoming a basket case. Still, I think it's better to be with someone rather than always being alone."

"I'm not getting an overwhelming urge to put on my clothes," Dean said. He was wearing a pair of Tony's pajamas. "So I wouldn't worry about me running out just yet."

"Well, I don't want to make you uncomfortable, but it would be great to just lie around, watch some football, take a nap. Do stuff," Tony said, with a wicked gleam in his eyes.

"Football? How butch! There's a dirty joke about a quarterback and a tight end somewhere in this conversation, but it's probably too obvious to mention."

Tony was about to respond when the doorbell rang.

"Who the hell could that be?" he asked as he made his way to the front of the house. Dean was making himself another cup of coffee when a familiar voice rang out behind him.

"Nice pj's, sweetie," Moose said, as he and Peter entered the kitchen. "We came over to get the dirt from Tony about your date, but clearly things went well. The sun is up and you're still here!"

Dean grumbled something under his breath. His friends knew him far too well. He hated being so predictable.

"So, how are we this morning?" Peter asked as he took one of the two seats at the large island that dominated the center of Tony's kitchen. They had brought a bag of muffins from a nearby bakery and were obviously not leaving anytime soon.

"Yes, how is the happy couple?" Moose asked.

Peter, who immediately recognized the look of panic on Dean's face, punched his husband in the arm. "I told you not to say the 'c' word. You're going to make Dean burst into flames."

"I fuckin' hate you two," Dean said, as he busied himself with cleaning the stove. Admittedly, he was freaked out about being called part of a couple. After all, they had just spent their first night together. He was just about to really start freaking out when Tony wrapped his arms around him.

"Don't let them get to you, baby," he whispered.

"Awwwww," Moose and Peter cried in unison.

Dean turned around and made a very obvious show of staring at the gorgeous set of Mauviel copper cookware that was hanging over the island. A couple of swift swings with a sauté pan and he knew he could solve all of his problems.

"I take it they don't often see you with someone?" Tony asked.

"No, and now you know why," Dean said.

"C'mon sweetie, we're just giving you a hard time," Moose said. "Of course, not the kind of hard time you probably had last night."

Wistful thoughts of the sauté pan momentarily drifted back into Dean's mind. Despite his annoyance at the intrusion, the four of them spent the next hour talking and laughing. It seemed like there was a new dynamic at work between them. They were two couples rather than 'Moose & Peter' and Dean. It was different and although he was probably imagining it, it seemed as if they enjoyed his company more when he was with Tony than without. Was that fair? Did couples prefer being around other couples or was he just in need of something new to worry about?

After Moose and Peter finally left, Dean and Tony went into the living room and threw themselves down on the couch. Much to Dean's surprise, he didn't leave until very late that evening. Even more surprising was that he didn't want to.

CHAPTER 17

Dean was still floating on air Wednesday evening when the second half of the bowling season began. The weather had turned mind-numbingly frigid. During their first winter in Chicago, he and Lonny could barely function. The two southern boys were not prepared for the absoluteness of the cold. That first winter, they made a vow that after they had spent a few years establishing themselves in their careers, they would get the hell out of Chicago and move to somewhere much warmer. As the years went on they adapted and they had never left. Dean had grown to love his adopted home but there were days like this one when his home sucked beyond comprehension.

As he entered the bowling alley, he felt the warmth rush over him. He walked over to the team sheet that was posted on the bulletin board, found his lane and made his way over. His face was beet red by the time he reached the lane, as the blood had finally decided to start flowing through his veins again. He shrugged off his heavy coat, and was just about to start untying his boots, when he was wrapped up from behind in a strong embrace. For just a fleeting moment, he thought it might be Tony. It wasn't.

"Hey sexy, where have you been keeping yourself?" Kurt asked, refusing to let Dean go. Bill ignored them and started taking off his coat and shoes.

"Oh, you know, here and there," Dean said, firmly removing Kurt's arms.

"We were looking for you at Sidetrack on Saturday night," Kurt said.

"Actually, I had a date with Tony on Saturday night."

"How'd it go?" Bill asked, suddenly much more interested in the conversation.

"It was awesome. He's a great guy and we had a lot of fun. I'm going to have him over for dinner this weekend."

Kurt was on the verge of saying something truly nasty when Moose and Peter joined the group. Peter sat next to Bill without taking off his coat, hat or gloves. Bill wrapped his arms around him and tried to warm him up.

"Hello boys," Moose said. "I need to drink a *lot* of beers tonight before heading back out into that shit. We had to park four blocks from here."

"No worries. The other team hasn't even shown up yet," Bill said. "Dean was just filling us in on his date with Mr. Wonderful."

"All I was saying was that Tony's coming over for dinner on Saturday night. I almost wish I hadn't invited him. My place can't even begin to compare to his."

"Tony doesn't really seem like the kind of guy who cares about that stuff," Moose said. "He really is one of the least pretentious guys I've ever met. And cute. And sweet."

"Whatever," Kurt said, before grabbing Dean again. "I hope this fling doesn't prevent us from getting another piece of you."

Dean extricated himself from Kurt's grasp once again. "Well, sorry, but it does. I can't date one guy and sleep with other people. I'm just not wired that way."

"Oh well, your relationships never last more than a couple of weeks anyway, so you'll be back on the market before you know it," Kurt said.

"Hey!" Moose yelled. "Don't be such a dick. Tony is nice. I think this is going places."

"Drop it, Moose," Dean said.

"You all are going to have to forgive my husband," Bill said coldly. "He's terrified of the notion that he'll have to spend more time alone with me."

The tension between Bill and Kurt had been bubbling over more and more in public, and now it was in full view. Everyone loved them, despite Kurt's sometimes brutish behavior, and didn't know what to do. Bill's comment put an end to the discussion, and they all busied themselves getting ready for what was apparently going to be a long night.

Fortunately, however, by the middle of the second game it seemed that all of their moods had thawed along with their bodies. It helped that they were beating the crap out of the other team. It helped even more that their opponents couldn't care less. They were the only lesbian team in the league and they were a blast to hang with. It was turning out to be a pretty good evening, Dean thought, in spite of the way it started.

He was just heading to the line to try and pick up a spare when he glanced up and saw Erik and Terrell heading toward their lane. Then he saw Tony right behind them. Deciding to avoid the introductions that would undoubtedly be laced with mild drama, Dean went to bowl while everyone said their hellos.

Completely flummoxed by Tony's sudden appearance, Dean threw a gutter ball. He hung his head in shame and made his way over to Tony.

"I blame you for that one," Dean said. He kissed Tony just enough so that he knew he was glad to see him, but not so much as to make a scene.

"Sorry about that," Tony replied. "We were having dinner nearby and decided to stop in and say hello. I hope you don't think I'm crowding you."

"Don't be silly. It's great to see you."

"I don't know quite how to tell you this Dean," Terrell said gravely. "But I don't think this thing between you and Tony is going to work out."

"Oh? Why is that?" Dean replied, still resting comfortably in Tony's arms.

"We had a very long talk at dinner. And, well, there's no easy way to put this, but I'm afraid Tony is a huge fan of modern art."

Shocked, Dean stepped away from Tony.

"It's true, I'm terribly sorry. They were telling me that you weren't such a fan. We're going to have to work on that."

"Take it from those of us who have known Dean much, much longer than you, if it was painted anytime after Van Gogh died, he isn't going to like it," Kurt said. He walked up behind Dean and hugged him tightly to his chest before continuing. "So, dating Dean, attending everyone's parties, dinner with Erik and Terrell...you're becoming quite the regular around out little group."

"And we're all thrilled about that," Moose said, giving Kurt the evil eye as he dragged him away from Dean and Tony.

"Sorry about that," Dean said, his mood darkening a bit.

"Don't worry about. He seems like an unhappy guy."

"Amen to that," Bill muttered, heading up to the line.

"Well, I suppose if there weren't any claws bared, it wouldn't be gay bowling," Dean said with a laugh, before burying his head in Tony's chest.

Dean was just about to say something else, when he saw someone several lanes down trying desperately to get his attention. He and Tony both looked over to see a small, odd looking man of indeterminate race waving at Dean and frantically pointing at his scoreboard.

Dean smiled and started to head toward the jumpy little man. "I'll be right back."

"Who is that?" Tony asked, to no in particular.

"Oh, that's Dean's last lover, Kishi Wu," Kurt said, drawing laughter from everyone.

Peter decided to fill Tony in on the story. "Kishi is sort of infamous around here. For the longest time, he couldn't find a team to join. Every week, he would show up hoping to be a substitute on someone's team if they were short a player. It was sort of the anti-lottery, because he's just so strange and he can't bowl to save his life."

"That's not exactly true," Bill said. "He got a strike on our lane once. Of course, he was bowling from the next lane over."

"Anyway, not only does he look kind of odd but when he starts trying to interact with you, well, let's just say he's one of those people with no social skills. So one night last season, Moose and I were on vacation and the team had to find a sub or forfeit the night. They got stuck with Kishi."

"Oh God, don't remind me," Kurt said.

"Well, that night, apparently no one on either team was really talking to him and he would just end up standing alone, fidgeting in the background. Dean felt bad and started trying to draw him out. Kishi pretty much fell head over heels after that. Anyway, long story short, Dean let him down easy, helped him find a permanent team and is just very nice to him."

Dean returned as Bill finished was finishing his story.

"What did I miss?" Dean asked, as the snickers began to die down.

"They were just giving me further proof, not that I needed it, that you're one hell of a guy," Tony said, kissing Dean softly on the cheek.

"Nah, I'm nothing special," Dean said, blushing furiously and thanking the heavens that it was once again his turn to bowl.

"Try to keep it out of the gutter this time, sweetie," Peter said.

Moose managed to keep Kurt in line for the rest of the evening, and Tony, Erik and Terrell stayed until the team finished. Everyone decided to head to a local bar for one or two more drinks, but Dean begged off, having another early day to face in the morning. Tony decided to stay with Dean, prompting everyone else to leave with giggles and sexual innuendos galore. After he stowed his gear in his locker, Dean and Tony made their way into the cold night air. Tony took Dean's hand as they walked, and Dean immediately felt a great deal warmer inside.

"Have I mentioned how much I'm looking forward to Saturday night?" Tony asked.

"No, you haven't, but I'm glad. I should warn you though, my place isn't quite as grand as yours. I lead a pretty simple life."

"Is there a kitchen?"

"Of course"

"Is there a bed?"

"Yes, but not as big as yours. We may have to snuggle closer."

"Then I think we're going to be fine," Tony said, with a wink at Dean, who was now shivering in the cold. Tony pulled him closer and held him tight.

They walked the five blocks to Dean's apartment at a very brisk pace and were breathing hard through burning lungs by the time they reached it.

"Do you want to come up and warm up for a bit?" Dean asked, hoping Tony wouldn't take it as a come on.

"Do you really have a busy day tomorrow?"

"Yeah, why?"

"Let's just say that if you want any sleep, I'd better say my goodnight here," Tony said, before putting Dean's hand on his crotch. Dean could feel the heat and the hardness through his gloves.

"I cannot believe that you're hard. That shouldn't even be possible in this weather."

"It must be the company," Tony replied, before kissing Dean. "Now I really need to go, or the decision is going to be taken completely out of our hands and I'm trying very hard to be a gentleman."

Dean watched him go and realized that Tony wasn't the only one who was generating heat south of the border.

CHAPTER 18

Over the years, Lonny had held many jobs. He had been a waiter, a bartender, a bookseller, a lifeguard, and even, for a very brief time, an architectural tour guide in Chicago. But the job that he had held the longest, by far, was that of the guy who frequently had to talk Dean down off an emotional ledge. By six PM on Saturday, Dean had become convinced that his night with Tony was going to be an unmitigated disaster. He had already been in the kitchen for two hours and nothing was remotely close to being finished. He had Lonny on the wireless earpiece so they could talk while he prepared a meal that he was certain would be inedible.

"I swear to god, if these onions don't start browning, I am going to go absolutely apeshit," Dean muttered. It was unclear if he was talking to Lonny or the uncooperative Vidalias slowly sautéing in the pan.

"Well, that's what you get for using something from Georgia," Lonny replied. He was loathe to admit he lived in the south, even if Florida could hardly be considered the real south. It bordered Georgia and Alabama, so he felt a certain amount of guilt by association. "Besides, who serves onions during a romantic dinner?"

"They are caramelized onions," Dean said, as if that should clear up any questions that a sane human being might have.

"I don't care if they're magic onions. You're still going to fart in your sleep."

"Thank you so much for that. I do not fart in my sleep."

"Oh, honey, please. We used to go camping together, remember? I swear there were some nights when I would have risked getting eaten by a bear just to escape the foul stench coming from your sleeping bag."

"Lonny, I swear you're on my last nerve. That was twenty-five years ago and we ate nothing but beans and franks for a week."

"Whatever you say, DeeDee, but I still think it's a big risk."

"You're not helping."

"What on earth are you worried about? You're the best cook any of us has ever known. Tony is crazy about you. It's not like anything could possibly go wrong."

"Are you trying to jinx me?"

"Jesus, Dean. Relax."

"You didn't see his place. It was amazing. He's going to come here to my little one bedroom apartment and wonder what the hell he's doing with me."

"You know, honey, not everyone is as shallow as you are," Lonny joked, knowing full well that Dean was the least shallow person he had ever known. Overly concerned with appearances, yes, but that was more about his insecurities than shallowness. "Did it ever occur to you that Tony just likes you because you're you?"

"No, that can't be it."

"Whatever. I'm tired and I don't want to indulge this whiny side of your personality any longer. I want you to promise me something before I hang up."

"What?"

"Just relax and try to have a good time. You like him, he likes you, and it's going to be fine."

"I will try," Dean said.

"Good boy. One more thing?"

"Yes?"

"Did you remember to shave your legs?"

"Goodbye Lonny," Dean said, laughing in spite of himself.

"I'm kidding. Did you remember to shave your balls?"

With that, Dean ended the connection. He really did need to lighten up. He looked at the clock and saw that he had almost an hour until Tony arrived. A quick survey of the kitchen told him that the meal was actually coming along better than he realized. Maybe he was stressing himself out for no reason.

He had completely forgotten about the earpiece he was wearing moments after he had hung up on Lonny, which is why it scared the shit out of him thirty seconds later when it rang again.

"Hello?"

"I'm very excited!" Moose said.

"Why is that?" Dean asked distractedly, as he began to trim the asparagus.

"Because of your date, silly."

"Why? Are you coming?"

"Well, not as much as you guys will be."

"Is there is purpose for this call other than to annoy me?"

"Lonny called and said you were bored and just hanging out and that I should give you a call and occupy you for the next hour or so," Moose said, innocently.

"You know, it occurs to me that maybe the reason I've been single all these years has more to do with the *help* I get from my friends than any shortcomings that I might personally have."

"Oh no, honey, it's definitely because of you. Anyway, what are you making?"

"I'm keeping it simple. I don't want it to seem like I'm

showing off. I picked up a nice roast fillet of beef, the garlic cheddar mashed potatoes are baking, I'm working on the asparagus with lemon sauce, and then later I'm making my molten lava chocolate cake with raspberry sauce."

"Oh, yeah, that's simple. Let's see, garlic, cheddar, lemon, and chocolate. I'm pretty sure I know what wine I'd choose, but what flavor condom goes with all of that?"

"You know, I'd love to continue this, but my call waiting just kicked in, so sorry," Dean said, quite happy to click over to the incoming call. "Hello?"

"Hey, it's Peter. Lonny says you're bored."

"How can you be on the phone? I just hung up on Moose."

"It's called a cell phone, sweetie. I swear they are going to be the next big thing."

"Why are you two tormenting me?"

"Because it's so much fun," Peter said, stating the obvious.

"Really? For whom, exactly?"

"For us, of course. Don't be dense."

"On that note, I really do have to finish this meal. However, please keep in mind that at some point in the near future, when you and your sewer-dwelling husband least expect it, I will pay you back for this. Love you!" Dean said, hanging up over Peter's protest on the other end.

They were quite the group, his friends. It was a little disturbing how excited everyone was about his date. Again, the thought crept into his head that they somehow thought less of him because he was single. Was it that they were worried about him being alone or did they just think that he was somehow pathetic? Not for the first time, he began to marvel at how much the gay community had changed over the years. When did everyone decide that settling down in a relationship was the way it was supposed to be? He was just about to start working on the lemons - and worrying about how his friends really felt about him - when the phone rang again.

"What?" Dean yelled.

"Um, hi! It's Tony. I just wanted to know if you needed me

to bring anything over tonight."

After an embarrassing fit of laughter, Dean explained the hell that his friends were putting him through this evening.

"So, you see, it's not just a simple dinner date that we're having tonight. Apparently the romantic hopes and dreams of the entire western hemisphere are riding on this date," Dean said.

"So, red wine?" Tony asked, making Dean laugh again.

"You don't need to bring anything but yourself. I'll see you in a little while."

* * * * *

The dinner turned out to be fine, despite all of Dean's worrying. He and Tony had a wonderful time, just relaxing and enjoying each other's company. It occurred to him that he had rarely felt so at ease around someone that he was also romantically interested in. Usually when he liked someone he always felt like he was on a job interview, trying to put his best foot forward and never saying the wrong thing. But with Tony, he could relax, which had never really been his strong suit no matter what the situation. There was something about him that drew Dean out of his protective shell. He felt safe around him and didn't feel the need to keep up all of the barriers that he normally built up around himself.

Later that night, after another round of extraordinary sex, Tony again brought up the subject that Dean hated most of all.

"I know I've mentioned this before, but for the life of me, I can't believe you're still single."

"And for the life of *me* I don't understand why you keep obsessing over it," Dean said, more sharply than he intended.

"Hey, it was a compliment. I didn't mean anything by it."

"I know. I'm sorry. It's just that I don't understand why everyone makes such a big deal out of it. I know I don't play myself up much, but if I look at things objectively, I'm a pretty decent guy.

"I couldn't agree more," Tony said, wondering where Dean was going with this conversation.

"I've had to work for everything that I have, and believe me it hasn't come easily. I've put myself through college, I've made a pretty good life for myself. I've made a lot of mistakes along the way and there are a lot of things that I wish I would have done differently. I'm like anyone – I've got my good points and I've got my bad points. But on the whole, I think I'm an okay guy. Nothing spectacular, but okay.

"Well, I think you're a little more than just okay, but why split hairs," Tony said.

"My point is, shouldn't that be enough? Why does everyone feel the need to put an asterisk on my life that implies that just because I never found a husband, I'm somehow less of a person?"

"Wow. How long have you been holding that in?" Tony asked.

Dean laughed softly and put his head back down on Tony's chest. "You know, I feel like I can say anything to you, but I might need to start filtering a bit."

"Dean, I think a lot of things about you, but I've never thought of you as less of a person because you're single. I'm kind of grateful that you're single," Tony said.

"It's like owning a home," Dean said, drawing a look of confusion from Tony. "Everyone I know owns their own home and they always ask me why I'm still renting. Nobody knows why, but they all assume it's because of some failure on my part. Like I'm out blowing my money or something. It just seems like everything is a competition sometimes. I was actually dreading you coming over tonight, because I was afraid I would get the same thing from you."

"But you didn't, did you? I don't care about all of that stuff, Dean. I know I have a lot. I don't feel bad about it, but I don't rub it in people's faces either. I've been luckier than most people in some areas and unluckier in others. Life just shakes out that way."

"Well, to be honest, I feel like I've been unlucky in most areas. Not to sound overly dramatic, by my life has been a struggle in so many ways. I don't think my friends really get that. I just hate the idea that people think less of me when I would never think any less of them, no matter what their circumstances."

"Listen, I haven't known you for that long, and I don't know your friends as well as you do, but I never get that impression from them. Everyone seems to think the world of you. I know that I do. You seem to have an inner strength that seems to be lacking in most people. I wish you could see that. You're a good man, Dean. I think that makes you pretty special."

Dean settled back down into Tony's embrace. He liked that Tony thought so highly of him, but at the same time, there was a part of him that just couldn't quite believe it. Maybe it wasn't his friends' opinion of his life that was the problem, but his own.

CHAPTER 19

Two weeks later, and against Dean's better judgment, he and Tony were on their way to Moose and Peter's house to join them, Kurt and Bill for dinner. Moose had a never-ending need to make sure everyone in their circle of friends was happy. He knew that Tony and Kurt didn't particularly care for each other and he was determined to make them become friends. He had broached the idea to Dean over one of their work-week lunches and after much arm-twisting had convinced him that it was a necessary evil. Moose was certain that the more Kurt saw them together as a couple, the more he would come to realize that his days of pursuing Dean were over.

As Tony pulled on to Lake Shore Drive, Dean took his hand and kissed it. "Thanks for coming tonight. I know this probably won't be the highlight of your week."

"What do you mean?" Tony asked.

"Oh, come on, I know that you don't like Kurt."

"Well, I like all your other friends, that has to count for something."

Dean laughed. "I know he can be a bit much sometimes, but he really is a good guy. Deep down. Way deep down."

"I'm sure he's nice enough," Tony said, choosing his words carefully. "And I know that you guys have a history. I also know that he wants more of you. But he needs to respect the fact that you and I are involved. I know it's only been a few weeks, but we *are* involved."

"I made it very clear to Kurt and Bill that the three of us weren't going to be messing around anymore. I'm sure they'll find another plaything soon and they'll forget all about me."

"Bill doesn't seem to be the problem. It's Kurt that I don't trust, to be perfectly honest."

"Well, trust me then. Kurt can hope for whatever he wants, but it isn't going to happen."

When they arrived at Moose and Peter's house, Kurt and Bill were already there, drinks in hand. As they took off their coats, Dean and Tony made the obligatory round of hugs and kisses.

"I told Kurt to behave tonight," Moose whispered to Dean as gave him a kiss on the cheek.

Dean's hopes for a drama-free evening were raised by Moose's comment, and then dashed just as quickly when Kurt grabbed his ass in full view of everyone as he kissed him hello.

"Let's all head into the kitchen," Peter said. "That's where the booze and munchies are."

When they reached the kitchen, Dean made himself a strong drink and planted himself next to Tony and as far as possible from Kurt.

"Did you guys get your invitation to Terrell's show?" Peter asked no in particular.

"Yes. Can't wait. Dozens of pretentious queens standing around trying to convince me that three marshmallows glued to barbed wire is art," Dean said.

"Hey! We're some of those pretentious queens you're talking about," Moose said.

"In case you'd forgotten Dean isn't really a fan of modern

art," Bill said to Tony.

"Despite what you guys think, I do like some modern art," Dean said, "Just not stupid modern art. I like some of Terrell's older stuff, but the things he's been doing lately – I don't know what the hell he's thinking with that shit. Give me the Dutch realists any day. That was art."

"I love the classics too," Tony said. "But modern art feels more immediate to me."

"Well, I'm sure you'll love it then," Dean said, quickly downing half of his newly made drink. "You can chat with the aficionados and I'll just stand there and try not to yawn."

"Enough about art. Let's talk about the lovebirds. We haven't seen much of you boys lately," Kurt said to Dean and Tony. "Still going at it like bunnies? Of course, Dean has the sweetest ass I've come across in a long time – no pun intended – so I can't say as I blame you."

"Well, we're managing to squeeze in the little things like work, eating, and breathing," Dean said. He was trying to keep things light, but the look on Tony's face told him that it wasn't working.

"Actually, it's been great. It's been a long time since I dated someone that I like this much," Tony said, as he kissed Dean on the forehead, before looking directly at Kurt. "I'd almost forgotten how good it felt to just *be* with somebody. But, of course, you guys have all been couples for years, so I'm sure you know what I mean."

"Oh, don't worry, that feeling will pass after awhile," Kurt said. "Well, maybe not for you two. You guys have been going out for what, three weeks now? You're approaching Dean's standard half-life on relationships. Tick tock."

Guests or no guests, Peter could sense that his husband had just about reached the limits of his patience with Kurt. Especially since he had just managed to insult Bill, Dean and Tony in one fell swoop.

"Okay, as much as fun as this is, I need some of you out of the way if I'm going to finish dinner," Peter said, doing his best to throw a life preserver to an evening that was quickly going under. "Dean, why don't you and Tony help me in here? Kurt, Bill, you go help Moose set the table."

Kurt was just about to protest when Moose grabbed him by the arm and escorted him out of the kitchen with a look that would have shamed most people on the spot. Of course, Kurt wasn't most people. Bill followed them out, with an oddly resigned smile on his face.

"Tell me again how deep down he's really a wonderful person," Tony said to Dean.

"If it's any consolation, I'm sure Moose is ripping him a new one as we speak," Peter said.

Dean remained quiet and started checking the meal that Peter was preparing. Why did everything have to be so complicated? He was beginning to think that Kurt had real feelings for him, and that just wouldn't do. He didn't want to mess things up with Tony and he didn't need any hassles from Kurt. Between work, Lonny, and his own issues, his life was already hectic enough without trying to manage the feelings and egos of his friends and the man he was starting to fall for.

"Are you okay?" Tony asked.

"Yeah, I'm fine. I just wanted to have a nice evening and it doesn't seem to be in the cards. Life should be easier."

"Well, maybe it would be if you hadn't slept with them," Tony said, regretting it as soon as it was out of his mouth.

"Yes, thank you for pointing that out."

"I'm sorry, I shouldn't have said that. That was an asshole thing to say."

"I'm not going to argue with you on that one," Dean said. He downed the rest of his drink and went to the freezer to get more vodka.

"How are things in here," Moose asked, as he rejoined the group in the kitchen.

"Not good," Peter warned has he pulled some garlic bread from the oven.

Moose could see that something had happened between

Dean and Tony, and once again, his need for harmony forced him to speak up. "Look, don't let Kurt stir up trouble between you two. I just had a chat with him and he's going to be on much better behavior for the rest of the evening. Trust me."

"Oh, don't worry about him," Tony said. "It's me and my big mouth that's the problem in here. Dean just got a glimpse of the jealous Italian side of me, and it wasn't pretty. Any ideas how I can get him to forgive me?"

"Hmmm, chocolates. Hmmm, chocolates. He's a big fan of chocolates," Peter said.

"And romantic movies," Moose chimed in. "I know he seems butch, but pop in a Reese Witherspoon or Sandra Bullock DVD and he'll weep like a school girl."

"But don't give him flowers, he hates flowers," Peter said, clearly enjoying the teasing they were dishing out. "But he does like cards. Sweet, goofy cards. With puppies on them. Dean's a softie when it comes to puppies."

"Are you three about through?" Dean asked, doing his best not to smile.

"That depends, are you going to make nice with your boyfr...um, your Tony?" Moose asked.

"No permanent damage done," Dean said, as he walked over and kissed Tony on the cheek. A look of relief washed over Tony's face and he wrapped his arm around Dean's waist and pulled him close.

* * * * *

True to Moose's word, the rest of the night passed uneventfully. Kurt behaved himself to the best of his abilities and everyone seemed to let the bitterness of the early part of the evening fall by the wayside. The only fallout for Dean was that he couldn't quite get past what Tony had said to him in the kitchen. It was bad enough that he regretted sleeping with Kurt and Bill, he didn't need Tony throwing it in his face, as well. There were too many mistakes in Dean's past, and Tony would find out about most of them eventually. He wouldn't put up with the judgment. Not from Tony. Not from anyone.

"Listen, I want to apologize again for what I said in the kitchen," Tony said. He had been troubled by Dean's silence since they got in the car to drive back to Tony's house.

"Don't worry about it. Believe me, there will be times when I say things that I regret. I just want you to know that I'm aware that sleeping with them wasn't the best idea I've ever had. But I did it and that's that. I can't take it back."

"I know. What made me upset was the way he said it. It was demeaning to you. I think the world of you and I'll be honest, I can be very protective. If he keeps treating you that way, he and I are going to have a problem."

"He'll calm down eventually. If he doesn't, I'll talk to him. We'll all get through this. My friends are important to me, and you're important to me too. It's not often that I have to balance those two things, so bear with me. It'll all work out."

"I guess I just like to think that I'm special," Tony said, taking Dean's hand as he drove. "I like to think that when we're together, I'm the one that matters most. I know it's silly, but there it is."

"You are special, Tony. I hope you believe me when I tell you that I really am a one man guy when I'm dating someone. But you also have to understand that I've lived in Chicago a lot of years. There are a few guys that we're going to run into that I've had sex with. Hell, more than a few. You were married all those years so we're probably never going to run into anyone that you've slept with. I just don't want to have to feel guilty every time some guy from my past pops up."

"And you shouldn't feel guilty. It's like I said before, I'm much more concerned about the present and the future. My insecurities just got the better of me tonight. Forgive me?"

"Absolutely," Dean said. They drove the rest of the way in silence, but it was finally a comfortable one. It dawned on Dean that he and Tony were on their way to an actual relationship. In the past, that sort of realization would have made him break out in a cold sweat and start planning escape options. But for some reason, thinking about a relationship with Tony filled him with a sense of calm that he had rarely felt before.

CHAPTER 20

For the first time in more years than he cared to think about, Dean was actually dating someone on Valentine's Day. Being single in a group of friends that was almost exclusively made up of couples was hard enough – being single at Valentine's Day was so much worse. All of his friends would talk about their romantic dinner plans and their gifts and their flowers while he would listen politely. Then, inevitably, they would ask what he was doing. Just as inevitably, his answer would be 'nothing.' They would tell him he should go out and meet someone. They would say that he should go to one of the bars that were having a Valentine's Day party. He hated February 14th with a passion that defied logic. It had finally reached the point where he just stopped talking to people in the days leading up to pre-fabricated event and just plowed his way through it. Still, it always hurt that he was alone. Despite his best efforts not to obsess about it, he always felt like he was missing out on something.

But for once, as Valentine's Day approached, he wasn't alone. He was dating a great guy. They had made plans for a romantic dinner. It was going to be perfect, and it was going to make up for all of those years where he sat home alone.

So, naturally, Tony came down with the flu.

To add insult to injury, Valentine's Day was on a Friday, which meant the entire weekend was shot.

"You're shitting me," Lonny said during their call on Friday morning.

"I shit you not," Dean said.

"You have the worst dating karma of any person I know."

"Thanks, that really makes me feel better."

"So what are you going to do?"

"Nothing, he's sick. He told me that he doesn't want to get me sick and that I shouldn't come over. We're going to try and do something next week."

"You're an idiot."

"Excuse me?"

"It's Valentine's Day and your boyfriend is sick. You don't just stay away. Make him chicken soup. Send him flowers. Do something. God, you're the worst dater ever."

"He told me stay away," Dean said defensively. "I'm just doing what he asked."

"He doesn't really want you to stay away. He needs pampering. And again, it's Valentine's Day. You have to do something."

"I seriously doubt that he wants me to show up on his door step when he's feeling like crap."

"Dean, trust me. That is exactly what he wants."

The argument went on for another half hour before he finally cut Lonny off and told that him that he had to go. Over the course of the day he had basically the same conversation with Moose, Terrell and Bill. By four o'clock, they had broken him down and he realized that he only had a few hours to figure out what he was going to do.

After leaving work and making a quick stop at the grocery store, he arrived home to find a large bouquet of flowers waiting by his front door. Clearly, everyone had been right.

Even battling the flu, Tony had managed to send him flowers. Dean opened the door, went inside, and set down the groceries and the suddenly inadequate bouquet of flowers that he had purchased before heading back outside to haul in the arrangement that Tony had picked out.

When he opened the wrapping, he was confronted with twelve long stem roses – six red and six yellow. The card said simply:

> Dean,
> *I know you hate flowers, but I hope you'll indulge me. This seemed like an appropriate mix of roses for something new – but something wonderful.*
> *Happy Valentine's Day,*
> *Tony*

Clever man, Dean thought. He only allowed himself a few seconds to admire the flowers, however, because there was much work to be done.

* * * * *

Two hours later, he waited nervously at Tony's front door. He had rung the bell twice, and was beginning to worry that Tony might be asleep. He was just about to give up and leave Tony a note when he heard movement coming from the other side.

To say that Tony looked like hell when he finally answered the door would have been a gross understatement. He obviously hadn't shaved in a couple of days, his hair was a disaster, and he was wearing a pair of sweatpants and an old t-shirt.

"No, no, no," Tony moaned, when he saw Dean at the door. "You were supposed to stay away."

"I brought homemade chicken soup," Dean said, as he held out a large bowl.

Tony smiled and Dean couldn't help but think that even now, Tony was the most handsome man he'd ever known. Since Dean's other hand was occupied with flowers, Tony opened the door and let him in.

"I'd kiss you, but I'd hate for you to get this," Tony said as Dean walked by and made his way to the kitchen. Tony followed slowly behind him.

"Well, as irresistible as you look right now, I think I'll hold off on that kiss for awhile."

Tony started laughing, which quickly turned into a coughing fit that would have sounded right at home in a TB clinic.

"Oh, that was hot," Dean joked.

"Don't make fun of me," Tony whined, in the way that only a man who is sick can whine. "What on earth are you doing here? You're too sweet for words, you know that?"

"Nah. I just wanted to make sure you were okay and had plenty to eat. Plus, my friends let me know in no uncertain terms that it's acceptable to disregard anything said by the man you're dating if he's sick."

"I'm sorry I ruined Valentine's Day."

"Oh stop it. And sit down."

Dean grabbed a pot from over the island, transferred the soup into it and began heating it up on the stove. Once it started simmering he walked over to Tony and placed his hand on his forehead to check his temperature.

"Doesn't seem too bad," Dean said. He lingered by Tony, stroking his hair.

"Yeah, I think the worst of it was last night. That was not pretty at all."

"Well, for what it's worth, you don't look so bad. The stubble is kind of hot actually."

Tony started laughing quietly.

"What's so funny?"

Tony stretched out the fabric of his sweatpants so that it was flush with his skin. The outline of his erection was easy to see.

"You are a freak of nature," Dean said, with a laugh.

"I can't help it. You turn me on."

Dean went back to the stove to check on the soup. After giving it a couple of stirs, he started searching through the cabinets for a vase. Once the flowers were taken care of, he set the table with soup bowls for himself and Tony. Of course, he had to lift Tony's head up off the table in order to make room. After filling the bowls, he sat down opposite Tony and smiled.

"Bon appetite," he said.

"Dean, this really is the sweetest thing anyone has done for me in a long time."

"It's my pleasure. But don't get any ideas. As soon as we're done with dinner, you're going back to bed – and I'm leaving."

"Awww...no snuggling?"

"No. I want you to sleep."

"I sleep great with you. It's nice to roll over in the night and know that you're there."

"Truth be told, I've always had the hardest time sleeping with other people," Dean said. "But with you, it seems to work pretty well. Still, as much as I'd love to stay, you're like a walking germ warfare lab right now."

"True," Tony said. "Oh my god, this soup is amazing. I think I can breath again."

"Yeah, I spiced it up a bit. I thought it might help clear you up."

Tony reached across the table and took Dean's hand and they sat quietly, eating their dinner. During all of those years when Dean sat home alone on Valentine's Day, he had so many fantasies about what a wonderful, romantic, time he would have if he ever got lucky enough to be with someone as wonderful as Tony. None of his fantasies ever imagined the sick, disheveled, runny-nosed mess across the table from him. For whatever reason, Dean decided that the reality was much better than the fantasy.

CHAPTER 21

Hiding in the corner of an upscale art gallery in Streeterville, Dean nursed a glass of cheap red wine and mulled over a list of nine thousand places he would rather be. Terrell's show was a huge hit. The gallery was crawling with Chicago's art house crowd, some of the beautiful people, and more press than he would have expected. Terrell was becoming big, and he was happy for his friend. Still, he just didn't get it. Who knows, maybe that was the whole point? If everyone liked modern art then it wouldn't be cutting edge, it would be mainstream.

At least Tony seemed to be enjoying himself. Dean looked across the room and saw him deep in conversation with Terrell, Erik and a woman whose name escaped him, but had been introduced as an art critic for one of the newspapers in New York. Tony caught Dean's eye and waved. Dean could see that he was excusing himself to join him. His thoughtfulness never ceased to surprise Dean.

"Are we having fun yet?" Tony asked.

"I swear this wine comes from a box," Dean said.

"Stop it. Seriously, you've had a chance to look around. What do you think?"

"I think the box this wine came in was cut up into pieces and thrown up on the wall."

Tony laughed loudly and drew a few disapproving looks from the nearby glitterati.

"Don't make me laugh like that or you're going to get us thrown out of here."

"A priest, a rabbi and a kangaroo walk into a bar," Dean began, before he was cut off by a kiss from Tony.

Dean was just about to try another joke cum escape attempt when he saw Kurt and Bill, along with Moose and Peter, heading their way. He and Tony had managed to avoid Kurt since the dinner at Moose's house, and he didn't want a repeat of what happened there. Tony followed Dean's gaze and turned to see the foursome approaching them. He instinctively wrapped his arm around Dean's waist as they arrived.

"Hello boys," Moose said. "Sorry we're a bit late. Fashion issues. We're surprised you're still here, Dean."

"The lengths I'll go to for my friends," Dean said, as he made a dismissive gesture towards the art on the walls.

"And how are you two?" Tony said to Kurt and Bill, deciding to break the ice.

"I've been told I need to apologize for last time. Sorry," Kurt said.

"That was very good, honey," Bill said. "Now let's see you roll over!"

"Oh, please! Since when was rolling over a problem for Kurt?" Peter said.

It wasn't perfect, Dean thought, but as the jokes continued, he could at least see the beginnings of a subtle shift within his circle of friends. It was obvious that enough people had come down on Kurt after their last encounter that he had finally gotten the message to back off.

"So listen, we're thinking of having everyone over for dinner the weekend after next," Bill said to Tony. "Are you two free?"

"Actually, no. I just found out this afternoon that I have to go to London on business. I leave Monday and I'm gone for a week," Tony said, before turning to Dean. "Sorry I didn't get a chance to tell you sooner."

"Fine, go. See if I care. They all leave eventually. They don't always feel the need to head for another continent, but whatever," Dean replied, with exaggerated hurt on his face.

"An ocean couldn't keep me away from you, baby," Tony said.

A round of groans, moans, and simulated vomiting followed as the long-term couples reacted to the antics of the relatively new lovers.

"I hope that wasn't directed towards my paintings," Terrell said, as he and Erik joined the group.

"Not at all. Emma and Mr. Darcy here were just expressing their undying devotion to each other," Moose said.

"Emma and Mr. Darcy weren't even in the same book," Dean said. "See, if you people would just skip back a couple of hundred years, you might actually get some culture."

"Are you saying that my husband's paintings and culture don't mix?" Erik asked.

Dean hadn't worked in the kiss-ass world of consulting for so many years without learning a thing or two and barely missed a beat before responding. "I think Terrell's paintings are unique and inspiring and wholly reflective of American culture in the early twenty-first century."

"You're continued support is a source of never-ending comfort," Terrell said dryly.

"I once spent a summer working on a farm," Bill said, drawing confused glances from everyone. "I think that was the last time I waded through so much bullshit."

Their laughter filled the room, but this time, since Terrell was with them, no one seemed to mind. It felt good to laugh with his friends again. He was amazed how much he had missed it. Between work, Tony's flu, and the incident with

Kurt, it seemed like the past few weeks had been one bit of bad luck after another. But now, with everyone together and having a good time, he could feel himself lightening up.

Yet another reporter wanted some time with Terrell, so he and Erik excused themselves. As the other two couples wandered off to view Terrell's work, Dean and Tony were left alone.

"God, I'm bushed. Let's go sit down for a minute," Tony said, guiding Dean to a seating area near the back of the gallery.

"So why are they sending you to London?" Dean asked as he sat down on a well-worn sofa.

"Another lawyer was supposed to be going there for a conference, but she broke her foot yesterday, so now I'm going."

"Nice. Free trip to London. Did you push her down the stairs or something?"

"Believe me I'd rather stay here. I've been so busy lately and this is just going to push me further behind. It's probably going to be a very exhausting trip. The conference is Tuesday through Thursday, but I extended my stay through the following Monday. I love London, it's a great city. You would really love it – especially the museums and the theater. It's just amazing."

"It's funny, I spent all those years traveling for work, so the last thing I wanted to do was get on a plane when I had any time off. I suppose when things calm down at work, I should take a trip over there. I've always wanted to see London. Oh, and Paris. I would love to go to Paris."

"Well, I can't do much about Paris right now," Tony said, pulling an airline ticket from his pocket. "But how would you feel about a long weekend in London?"

"What is that?"

"Let's see. Dean Davenport, Flight 498, Chicago to London, next Thursday night. It looks like a plane ticket to me."

"Tony, that's very sweet. But I can't accept that."

"Now before you start thinking of reasons to say no, let me say a couple of things. First, I used my miles, so it didn't cost a thing. Second, you'll take the red-eye over Thursday night and fly back with me on Monday, so you'll only miss two days of work – I think they can spare you for two days."

"Actually, they probably can spare me, but I can't let you do this. I have a ton of miles myself. Why don't you return the ticket and I'll book another one using my miles."

"It's a gift, Dean. If I wanted you to use your miles, I would have suggested it. But then it wouldn't have been a surprise. Besides, it was a small miracle that I was able to get a ticket at this late date. The fates want you to go. I want you to go. Hasn't anyone ever done anything nice for you? Again, I know this if difficult for you, but all you really need to do here is say thank you."

"Thank you," Dean said, smiling at Tony. "This is easily the sweetest thing anyone has ever done for me. You're a pretty great guy, you know that?"

"I'm just me. Lord knows I have my bad points – as you learned a few weeks ago. And part of this is pure selfishness. I really like you, and I like spending time with you."

Dean kissed Tony softly. They pulled back and stared at each other. Dean knew they were crossing a line from just dating into something deeper.

"What's that," Moose asked, as he and Peter squeezed onto the sofa next to Dean.

"Well, it seems I have the world's greatest boyfriend," Dean said, keeping his eyes on Tony and watching him smile at the use of the word boyfriend. "I'm apparently going to London next week."

"Get out!" Peter exclaimed, snatching the ticket from Dean's hands.

"Oh my god, that is so sweet," Moose said, painfully poking Dean in the chest. "This one is a keeper."

"You know something, you just may be right about that," Dean said.

CHAPTER 22

Dean and Tony were walking home from dinner on chilly, foggy, Sunday night in London. As Tony had predicted, Dean had fallen in love with the city. They had spent Friday and Saturday hitting the major sights, with especially long visits to the National Gallery and the Victoria & Albert Museum. On Saturday night they had managed to get last minute tickets for the latest bombastic musical in the Theater district. Earlier Sunday they had walked the halls and gardens of Hampton Court Palace.

Dean loved history and he had loved every minute of the trip. He loved it more because Tony was with him. He was still in awe of how they were when they were together. He knew it was a cliché, but he had never felt this way about anyone before. His feelings for Tony were deep, but they were balanced by a sense of serenity. The pace of the world just seemed to slow down a bit when Tony was near.

"What are you thinking about?" Tony asked, as he led Dean across the street on to Piccadilly towards the Park Lane Hotel, where they were staying.

"You. Me. Us. Me when I'm with you. This trip. I'm not looking forward to heading back to reality tomorrow."

"Reality isn't so bad, you know, if you have the right person to share it with."

"I'll remind you of that on Tuesday when you start answering the three hundred e-mails waiting in your in box," Dean said. He huddled close to Tony, trying to ward of the chill in the misty night air.

"Well, if it gets to be too much to bear, I'll just start thinking about getting to hold you again on Friday night. That always makes me feel better."

"It still amazes me to think that three months ago, I didn't even know you," Dean said. "I know I've said it a hundred times, but I want to thank you again for this trip. It's been great. There is so much that I want to do and see in my life, but I'm always too busy to think about it or, god forbid, actually go out and do it. I like sharing adventures with you."

"That's good to know, because I'm hoping there are going to be a lot more. There's still the whole rest of the world to see. But the real adventure is in the day-to-day stuff. The time just spent together. That's where the magic really happens."

"Do you write greeting cards in your spare time?" Dean asked, finding that he was still sometimes uncomfortable with Tony's intensity.

"Don't make fun. I'm serious."

"I know, I'm just teasing you. You're just so sincere sometimes that I can't help myself."

"And sincerity is a bad thing? I've been through some things in my life, too, you know. Love and loss both impact you in ways that you never expect, and they both make you grow. I like to think I have a pretty good handle on life and what I want out of it."

They found themselves in front of the Tower Records store. Dean was a fanatic for European pop music and had been dying to search through the store and see what he could take home with him.

"It's still open," Dean said. "Do you mind if we stop in for a bit? There are a couple of CD's I'm looking for."

"You can't see the beauty in a Jackson Pollock painting, but you can spend your hard earned money on British boy bands?"

"Don't judge me," Dean said, as he tried to pull Tony into the store.

"Actually, I have one last surprise up my sleeve," Tony said with a twinkle in his eye. "Why don't you take a look around here. I'm going to head back to the hotel and, um, do some stuff. Meet me in about half an hour?"

"What are you up to?" Dean asked, his affection for Tony battling with his need to be in control. Surprises were not his cup of tea.

"Trust me," Tony said. He kissed Dean on the cheek and then started walking quickly towards the hotel.

Dean stared after him for a bit and then went into the store, glancing at his watch. The hotel was about five minutes away, which gave him a decent amount of time to look around – and try to figure out what Tony was up to. Of course, he could just wait and see what would happen, but that just wasn't in his nature. That was the thing about being with someone that always caught him off guard – the realization that there was somebody else with his own needs, desires and ideas to take into consideration. He had been on his own for so long, and that was one of the hardest things for him when it came to relationships.

Lonny had once told him that the reason Dean was single wasn't because of the inevitable flaws, real or imagined, that he found in others, but rather that others had such a hard time getting close to him. He supposed it was true. It was far easier to be alone than to let someone in and then deal with the pain that came with eventually losing that person.

He was already starting to care deeply about Tony and occasionally thoughts would creep in to his mind about what would happen if they broke up. After losing his parents, and facing the prospect of losing Lonny, he sometimes wondered how much more he could take. Sometimes he wondered if he had the capacity to truly let anyone get close enough to get past the fear of losing them. He shook his head and reminded himself to focus on the good things. Besides, there was shopping to be done and time was wasting.

Thirty minutes later, and many pounds poorer, Dean reached the door of their spacious hotel room. He wasn't sure what surprise Tony had cooked up, but he was sure that he would enjoy it. If only he could figure out a way to hide the dozen CD's he had just purchased. He realized when he reached the door that Tony had taken the only key, so he knocked and waited.

"Hey there handsome," Tony said, as he opened the door. He was wearing one of the hotels bathrobes. "Come with me."

Tony rolled his eyes as he took the bag of CD's and tossed them on the bed. He then took Dean's coat off as well. Then, much to Dean's surprise, he kept undressing him – taking plenty of time to touch and caress each part of Dean's body as it was unveiled. When he was completely naked, Tony dropped his robe, pulled him close and kissed him passionately. As usual, their excitement mutual and instantaneous. Tony ended the kiss, took Dean's hand, and led him into the bathroom.

The bathrooms in most European hotels were incredibly cramped and utilitarian. Not so the Park Lane. The bathrooms in the larger rooms, one of which Tony had booked, were enormous. The bathroom was almost as big as the bedroom, with a sink, shower stall, heated towel rack, and most importantly, a very large bath tub.

Dean couldn't believe his eyes when he walked in. Dozens of candles were scattered around, making the room glow. Tony had moved the stereo into the bathroom as well, and Ella Fitzgerald was singing low and sweet. To cap it all off, he had prepared a scented bubble bath.

"Nice," Dean said. "Very, very nice."

"I thought you might like it."

"Are you always like this? I don't know if I can deal with this much romance on a consistent basis."

"I'm a romantic guy. What can I say?"

"And a horny one," Dean said, as he wrapped his hand around both his and Tony's dicks, slowly stroking them.

"Oh God, Dean. The way you make me feel. Come on," Tony moaned as he and Dean slid into to the tub.

Dean was pragmatic enough to realize that over time, the sexual energy between the two of them would fade somewhat. But so far, during the months that they had been together, the sex had always been extraordinary. It was as if Tony knew everything there was to know about Dean's body and how a touch here, or a lick there, could elicit the maximum possible pleasure. Dean, however, knew a thing or two about Tony's desires as well. And every now and then, Tony had his own itch that needed to be scratched. He had Tony pinned in the tub and thought there was no time like the present.

Dean kissed him and took him completely off guard by slowly sliding two fingers inside him. Tony gasped and moaned as Dean twisted, turned, and generally drove Tony insane. Dean saw the condoms and lube on the edge of the tub and it wasn't long before he had Tony up against the wall, riding him slowly, but forcefully. Their bodies moved in a comfortable familiarity, each knowing exactly what the other needed at that moment. Tony didn't get fucked often, and when he did, he didn't last long. When Tony climaxed, Dean had to hold his hand over his lover's mouth, just to make sure that no one called security.

A short while later, after Tony's mouth had produced an equally amazing orgasm for Dean, they settled back into the tub, which Tony and refreshed with hot water. Dean sank in Tony's arms and felt more at peace than he could ever remember.

"Now, see what you just shot up on the wall there? That's a Pollack-like thing of beauty that I can truly appreciate," Dean said.

"Yes, but is it art?" Tony asked, as he laughed and pulled Dean up, and nudged him to flip over. "I'm in love you with you, Dean."

It was simple and pure and Dean had utterly no idea how to react to it.

"Before you say anything, I want you to listen to me," Tony continued, before Dean could say anything. "I do love you. More that I ever imagined I could love anyone again. From the moment I first saw you, I think I knew that it was inevitable. Now, I want you to do something for me?"

"What?" Dean asked. He was suddenly off balance by the turn the evening had taken.

"I don't want you to say you love me. I don't want it to be a reaction. I want you to say it when you mean it. When you know it. When you feel it. I know that you're much more guarded than I am. Believe it or not, I'm okay with that. To me it means that when you do finally say it, you'll mean it with all of your heart."

"Tony, I don't know what to say."

"Well, you can start by telling me you're not completely freaked out."

"I'm not, *completely* freaked out. But you're right, I care for you deeply, but *love* – I'm afraid that I may not even know what that means anymore. It's been so long. I know that I've never felt this way about anyone before. When I'm with you, I feel safe and happy and wonderful."

"And that's enough for me, for now," Tony said. Much to Dean's amazement, he realized that Tony meant it. He wasn't rushing him or demanding an immediate commitment – he was just, quite simply, loving him.

Dean kissed Tony again, and then settled back around into his arms. He really couldn't remember a time when he'd felt this good. If it never got any better than this, it would be enough for him. But in the back of his mind, he could feel the old doubts start swimming their way to the surface. The doubts that said he was incapable of love, or more to the point, unworthy of it. It was a battle that he always fought with himself when he cared for someone. It was also a battle that he always lost. He had to wonder if his feelings for Tony would be strong enough to overcome the demons that had always held him back. He prayed they would.

CHAPTER 23

I t had taken forever to get through customs, but Dean and Tony were finally on their way home. They sat quietly in the cab, exhausted but happy. The traffic was stop and go, and the city was cold and overcast. It was a reality check that Dean felt was too soon in coming. As if to accentuate the feeling, his cell phone suddenly rang. His phone didn't work in London and he realized that he hadn't missed it. He recognized the number as Lonny's mother and his heart skipped a beat.

"Hello?"

"Hi Dean, it's Connie," she said, and Dean could sense the weariness in her voice.

"Hey Connie, is everything alright?"

"Didn't you get my messages?"

"No, I've been out of the country. It was a last minute thing and I just got back. What's going on?" Dean was suddenly terrified. He looked over and could see Tony watching him intently.

"Well, maybe that's for the best. The last few days have been quite a rollercoaster ride. Let me start by saying that

Lonny is okay. When you listen to my messages, you're probably going to hear some panic in my voice. As things were unfolding, it was a bit intense."

"Connie, what happened?"

"Lonny had a seizure on Friday night. We took him to the hospital and they couldn't get things under control. Finally, they realized that he had a blood infection. It's rare, but it happens. It was touch and go for awhile, but he's better now. He smacked his head on the table when the seizure hit, so they're doing some testing now to make sure there was no bleeding in his brain."

"Oh my god. Touch and go?" Dean asked. "Are you telling me that he almost died?"

"Dean, he's fine. We knew that as we got closer to the end, things would get more complicated. No one could have seen it coming. The good news is that he's alert and feeling mostly better."

"I should come down there."

"No, don't be silly, you just got home. He's fine, honey, I swear. They're going to keep him in the hospital for a few more days and then we can take him home."

Dean's mind was reeling. Was there never any peace? Did he have to pay for every moment of happiness with an offsetting moment of pain? His life was like a giant balance sheet, with the pluses and minuses ultimately equaling nothing.

"Dean, are you there?"

"I'm here," Dean said. "I just don't know what to say or do, Connie. I didn't imagine something like this happening."

"None of us did, honey. Please don't feel bad about this. Listen, he seems to be best late in the afternoon, so why don't you give him a call then, okay? He'd love to hear from you."

"Okay. Tell him I'll talk to him later."

"All right, Dean. I love you."

"You too," Dean said as he heard the click on the other end.

"What happened?" Tony asked, gripping Dean's hand and

trying to provide some amount of comfort.

Dean related what Connie had told him. There was a clinical distance in his voice, as if all of the emotion he had been feeling for the last few days had been sucked out of him.

"I'm sorry, Dean, I really am. I know this isn't easy, and that it will probably become even harder from here, but I just want you to know that I'm here for you. Okay?"

"Yeah, thanks," Dean said, but he was barely listening. "I can't believe that I didn't check my fucking messages."

"He was fine when you left, and you were only gone a few days. There was no reason to think anything would happen, it was just one of those things."

"He almost died – don't minimize it."

"I'm not trying to minimize it, I swear. It's just that as hard as it is, you need to focus on the fact that for right now, Lonny's fine," Tony said. He spoke with the authority that only someone who had lost someone could.

"He's dying. He's not fine. He's never going to be fine."

For the rest of the cab ride, Tony refused to let go of Dean's hand. But he could feel the walls going up around him. He recognized it because he had done the same thing when Steve had died. Everyone tried to help and everyone said all of the right things. But in the end it was Tony, alone with his grief, who had to deal with it. Still, the presence of others had helped, even if only in a small way. Hopefully, Dean would get something out of just knowing that Tony was there for him. But Dean wasn't Tony. And as much as he loved him, or maybe because of how much he loved him, that thought scared Tony very much.

* * * * *

Several agonizing hours later, Dean sat alone in his apartment, trying to find the courage to call Lonny. The fear surprised him. He had known for some time that he was going to lose Lonny. He knew that it wasn't an 'if' but rather a 'when.' But it wasn't until today that it became real. Lonny was going to die. Soon. In a few weeks or a few months, the man who was closer to him than a brother; the man who had been through everything with him since they were children, would be gone. Dean stared at the phone and couldn't bring himself to dial the numbers, as if postponing the call would also postpone the inevitable. But it wouldn't, and he knew it. So he dialed.

"Hello, Laddy," Lonny said, doing his best to sound cheerful. "How was London?"

"Screw London, how are you?"

"I'm fine DeeDee. I actually feel surprisingly well, all things considered."

"Lonny, I'm so sorry that I wasn't here. If I'd have known I never would have gone."

"Hell, I didn't know this was going to happen. I'm fine, Dean, really. Tell me about London."

"London was nice. We had a good time," Dean said, noncommittally.

"Uh oh, what happened?"

"What happened? Are you kidding me? I was off living it up in London when my best friend almost died. What the hell do you think happened? I can't believe I didn't even call once."

"You were gone for four days, lighten up."

"Have you met me?" Dean asked.

"True, lightness isn't exactly your forte, but some old dogs, even really old ones like you, can learn new tricks," Lonny replied, grateful that Dean had stopped the self-flagellation, if only for a moment. "Now, seriously, how was the trip?"

"Tony told me that he was in love with me."

"Oh, I'm sorry sweetie," Lonny said, as he laughed.

"Shut up, it's not funny."

"I know. It's quite sad, actually. Those are the magic words that make all of your relationships vanish in a puff of smoke. Did you break up with him right then, or has your devious little mind started planning for a better way to do it?"

"Well, I clearly don't have time for a relationship right now. Look at what happened this weekend. Not to mention that I'll be behind at work for the rest of the week."

Lonny had only been joking about Dean already looking for a way out of his relationship with Tony, but he suddenly had the feeling that he wasn't that far off the mark.

"Heaven forbid that you let your work suffer because of your personal life. And don't you dare use me as an excuse for you not having a relationship," Lonny said.

"I'm serious. If I hadn't been in London, I would have been here for you. Friends are way more important than lovers. I've always said that and this weekend just highlights how true it is," Dean said.

"The only reason you've always said that is because you've never actually had someone you were truly in love with. I think you might find that there is room in your life for both your friends and a husband."

"Well, you can be damn sure that I won't be leaving the fucking country any time soon."

"So when do I get to meet this guy?" Lonny asked, changing the subject and taking Dean completely off guard.

"What do you mean?"

"I mean when do I get to meet him? You didn't think that I was going to let you go off and marry someone without my approval, did you?"

"Lonny, we're not getting married. We've only been going out three months. He's the one pushing things along, not me."

"Putting your craziness aside for the moment, I still want to meet him. Why don't you two come down in a couple of weeks? Just for the weekend. I'm sure Mom won't mind if you share a room, so long as he doesn't bang your noggin against the head board too loudly."

"Shut up," Dean said, feeling his mood lighten ever so slightly. "I am not having sex in your mother's house."

"So I can tell Mom that you guys will be coming, so to speak?"

"I'll talk to Tony and see what his schedule is like, if it's really that important to you," Dean said.

"It is. Now, tell me all about London and don't leave anything out."

They talked until Lonny's cell phone battery started to give out. Dean told him everything about the trip and Tony and how he was feeling about their relationship. Lonny, for his part, listened, teased, and generally told Dean he was crazy for having any doubts. Lonny wasn't long for the world, and still it was he who was guiding and comforting Dean, rather than the other way around. They both knew it, and they both knew that it was the way it had always been between them. And though they didn't say it to each other, neither one of them knew how Dean would get along once Lonny was gone.

CHAPTER 24

Dean was so drained by Friday afternoon he could barely function. The trip to London, while wonderful, had been exhausting. He hadn't been sleeping well since his return, mostly because thoughts of Lonny and Tony whirled around in his mind whenever his head hit the pillow. Work had been an utter disaster all week and he had been putting in twelve hour days since his return. As he glanced at his calendar for the following week, he saw that things weren't going to get better any time soon. The semi-annual Board of Directors meeting was in six days and he was spending every free minute that he had trying to prepare for it.

Work, Tony, Lonny. His life seemed consumed by those three things, and even then, he needed to find time for his other friends and time for himself. Moose had wanted to have lunch during the week, but Dean just couldn't get away from work. He just didn't understand how other people did it. How did they make room for so many things when there seemed to be so little time to go around?

If there was a silver lining to the seemingly perpetual gray cloud that was shadowing him, it was that Lonny was doing a little better. His doctors had released him from the hospital Thursday morning, finally confident that the infection had been eradicated. Lonny actually sounded like his old self during their morning call, and it briefly lifted Dean's spirits. At the very least, he knew that he didn't have to start thinking about the end just yet, which was good, since he couldn't bear to.

He was about to head across the hall to have a conversation with his boss about the Board meeting when his phone rang. Looking at the caller ID, he could see that it was Tony. A week ago, he would have lit up like a Christmas tree, but in the mood he was in now, it just seemed like a burden.

"Hey there," Dean said.

"Hey, yourself, handsome," Tony said, bright and chipper as ever. "How's your day going?"

"It's okay. I'm glad it's Friday. Mind you, I'm taking work home this weekend, but I guess working at home in my boxers is better than working at my desk."

"MMM...I'll say. So do you want to grab some dinner tonight?"

"Honestly, Tony, I'm too tired. I just can't tonight. I probably won't get home until around eight. I wouldn't be good company anyway."

"Oh, that's okay. How about tomorrow then? I can cook and we can stay in and watch a movie or something."

Dean hesitated. Part of him wanted to see Tony, but part of him was overwhelmed. Not just by Tony, by everything. Unfortunately, Tony was the only thing he could control. He could have just been honest and told Tony what he was feeling, but as usual, he took the easy way out.

"Do you mind if we just play it by ear?" Dean asked. "I really do have a lot of work to do this weekend."

"Sure, Dean. I don't want you to feel like I'm crowding you or anything, I just want to see you."

"And you will, I promise," Dean said.

"Well, I won't keep you. I'll talk to you tonight, ok?"

"Actually, before you go, I wanted to run something by you," Dean said.

"Shoot."

"Lonny wants us to come down for a visit. Well, really, he wants to get to know you and give his stamp of approval. Just for a weekend. Maybe in a few weeks, if you're free."

"I'd like that a lot," Tony said. "I know how much he means to you. Just let me know the weekend and we'll book it."

"I'll book it, and we'll use my miles this time," Dean said. "That we'll be even."

"You're too much. There's nothing to be *even* with. The ticket to London was a gift. You don't owe me anything."

"Okay, okay," Dean said, not wanting to get into that again. "But we're still using my miles."

Tony just laughed. "I'll talk to you later, you goofball."

Dean smiled as he hung up the phone. He really did care for Tony, and more importantly, he liked the way that Tony made him feel. Maybe his life was too complicated right now, or maybe he was just using that as an excuse. He could only hope that Tony would stick around long enough for him to work through whatever was going on inside his head.

* * * * *

It was after eight when Dean finally made it home. He walked into his apartment, kicked off his shoes, threw off his coat and eased into the nearest chair. Looking around he realized that his place was a mess. Dishes were in the sink and clothes were strewn everywhere. He hadn't even bothered unpacking the suitcase from his trip to London. He knew he should get up and start cleaning and get the weekend off to a decent start, but he was just too tired. He closed his eyes and was asleep within minutes.

He rarely slept in the living room, which is why he jumped to his feet in confusion when his door buzzer started screeching. Caught off guard, he had no idea where he was or what was going on. After he took a moment to get his bearings, and after the damn buzzer stopped, he got his heart to slow down and went to answer the door.

"Yes?" Dean asked. His tone left no confusion as to his anger at being awoken.

"Well, hello to you too," Tony said, cheerfully.

"Oh, hey, come on up," Dean said. He thought he had been pretty clear when they had talked earlier in the day about wanting to be alone, but Tony obviously hadn't gotten the message – or didn't want to. There was a rap on the door and Dean tried to compose himself before opening it.

"Now, I know you said you wanted to be alone, and don't worry, I'm not staying long," Tony said, as he rushed by Dean into the apartment. "I just figured that you wouldn't feel like cooking, so I stopped and picked you up some dinner."

Dean was still standing by the door, holding it open and staring at Tony. He then looked around at his disaster of an apartment, closed the door and immediately started picking up clothes and papers and whatever else he could get his hands on.

"Tony, that's very sweet of you, but like I said, I'm just beat. I was actually asleep when you rang the bell," Dean said. His body was like an oil rig scooping up things as he talked.

"I know, and you can relax, I'm going to leave in a few minutes. I was out having dinner with my friend Rebecca, and I passed Chang's on the way and thought you might like not having to cook."

"That was nice of you. Thanks," Dean said. He had thrown all of the clothes into the hamper in the bathroom and made a beeline for the kitchen.

"What on Earth are you doing?"

"What do you mean?"

"Why have you suddenly become Hazel? Relax for minute."

"Well, I told you that I didn't want to get together tonight, so obviously I wasn't expecting company. Look at this place."

"Dean, seriously, you need to calm down," Tony said as he grabbed Dean by the shoulders and forced him to sit down. "Relax. What's the matter with you?"

"I just don't want you to think I'm some kind of slob. I've been so busy since we got back from London that I haven't had a chance to clean this place."

"You can't possibly think that I care if your apartment is a little bit messy."

"You may not care, but I do. That's one of the reasons that I didn't want to get together tonight. My life is just a little bit out of whack right now and I need some time to get it together. Of course, all I managed to do was come home and pass out in the chair like a redneck."

"Dean, I love you. I love you for who you are – not who you think you are. I'd love to see you this weekend, but believe me, I'll live if it doesn't happen. The last thing I want is for you to start thinking of our time together as some sort of obligation. I swear I just stopped by tonight because I thought you might be hungry. It's called 'doing something nice.' No strings, no ulterior motives."

Dean just stared at Tony, finding himself amazed again by the total lack of pretense in the man. Then he kissed him, hoping that his touch would convey what his words couldn't.

"You must think I'm completely bipolar," Dean finally said.

"I think you're very, very stressed out. And again, I don't ever want to be a source of that stress. I'm going to go and if you have time this weekend, let's get together. If not, we'll do something next week. Is that cool?"

"Totally cool. Thanks for being so understanding" Dean said, as he walked Tony to the door. He gave him one last kiss, and then Tony was gone.

He closed the door and sighed. Well, I must look like an utter lunatic now, he thought. He wished he knew how Tony managed to always seem so together. Other than the night of their first date, he had never seen Tony out of sorts. Their jobs were both stressful, they both had commitments outside of work, and yet Tony just seemed to sail through life while Dean felt like he was constantly struggling. A part of him resented Tony for that, even though he knew it was unfair. Hard to hold it against your boyfriend that he isn't as unstable as you are. Still, a part of Dean had to wonder how long it would take before Tony realized that he wasn't everything Tony thought he was cracked up to be.

CHAPTER 25

Much to Dean's surprise, his life did seem to calm down a bit over the following weeks. The Board meeting went off without a hitch. Dean wasn't sure if it was because of or in spite of his obsessing over it. He also managed to find more time for Tony, which made both of them happy. Still, he knew that something had changed between them since their time in London. He liked to think that it was just the constant stress of dealing with work and worrying about Lonny and the general pressures of life, but he knew better.

It was the "I love you."

Those three little words that he has always thought he wanted to hear, but which in reality, had freaked him out as much as they always did. Tony was everything he had ever wanted, and yet he couldn't bring himself to return the declaration that he had made. Fear of commitment? Fear of losing him? Fear of being tied down? He wished he knew.

It was Friday night and everyone had gathered at Erik and Terrell's house for cocktails before heading off to a Linda Eder concert at the Chicago Theater. Linda Eder performances were a long-standing tradition amongst Dean and his friends. They were gay after all. They had been attending her concerts since the days of the intimate Park West Theater. Over the years, she had become something of a gay icon and everyone still made it a point to make the time for her shows whenever she was in Chicago. Well, almost everyone.

"What do you mean you've never seen her in concert?" Moose asked, aghast and the sheer non-gayness of it all.

"I've just never seen her," Tony said. "I'm not even sure I know what she looks like. Is she the tall one?"

Moose turned to Dean. "I don't think I can process this."

"I know. I was as shocked as you are," Dean said, as he polished off his second drink. "When he told me, I thought he was kidding. But it's true. He's an Eder virgin."

"Well, we'll have you broken in before the night is over," Peter said, as he watched Tony watch Dean make himself another drink.

"I'm sure it will be great," Tony said distractedly. Dean's drinks seemed to have gotten stronger and more frequent in the past few weeks. Things weren't perfect between them, but they had been better lately. He just didn't understand why Dean was still drinking so much.

As Dean rejoined the circle of friends, Kurt wrapped his arm around his waist, pulled him closed, and kissed him on the cheek. He was being relatively good, but the growl he gave Dean let everyone know that he wanted more than just a chaste kiss. Much to Tony's disappointment, Dean didn't pull away.

"As I recall, it was after a Linda concert that the three of us made out for the first time," Kurt said.

"Oh my god, I'd forgotten about that," Dean said happily.

"Me too," said Bill, with nowhere near the happiness of Kurt and Dean.

Erik approached the group with some pamphlets and pulled Dean away to discuss the new kitchen that he and Terrell wanted to install. Peter, Kurt and Bill wandered off to find

Terrell, leaving Tony alone with Moose. They both seemed lost in their own thoughts.

"So, we haven't seen you since you got back from London," Moose said, breaking the silence. "Did you have fun?"

"It was pretty great. We really had a wonderful time. It was nice to be away from everything."

"I hope by everything you don't mean us."

"No, you guys are great. Just...everything. I'm worried about Dean. He seems so stressed out. And his mood is all over the place – up one minute, down the next. I'd like to think that I'm helping him, but sometimes I feel that I'm just one more annoyance in his life."

"Don't be silly, you're the best thing that has happened to him in forever. He's crazy about you. Unfortunately, he's also just a little crazy. Dean is a great guy, but he's wound so tight and takes so much on himself that sometimes I think it overwhelms him. Honestly, though, I think you help him cope."

"Actually, I think the booze is helping him cope lately."

"I wouldn't worry too much about that. It's something we've all noticed over the years. When he gets stressed, he drinks. Dean always needs to be in control, you know that. So when things get out of control, he drinks a bit more than usual. I think it's the only way he can allow himself to loosen up. Does that make sense, or did I just call him an alcoholic?"

Tony laughed. "No, it makes sense. I certainly don't think he's an alcoholic. I just wish he would lean on me a bit more, and the vodka a bit less. And show a little more sensitivity to our relationship. London was so fantastic, but I think I might have fucked it up while we were there."

"What do you mean?"

"I told him I loved him."

"Wow. I had no idea. He didn't tell me," Moose said.

"I'm not surprised. He seems to have pulled back since then. Maybe I'm moving too quickly for him."

"Don't be silly. You could have said it a year from now and it still would have thrown him for a loop. You have to understand, Dean has been alone so long that I was beginning to wonder if he'd every meet anyone that he really cared about. But I can see the way he looks at you Tony, he's crazy about you. Just give him time."

"Oh, don't worry, I'm not going anywhere. I sometimes wish I could, but I'm not built that way. I love the little bastard."

Moose and Tony's laughter caught Dean's attention. He looked at them quizzically, knowing they were probably talking about him. He and Erik joined them, just as everyone else came back in from the living room.

"By the way, did everyone get the directions to the cabin that I emailed yesterday?" Tony asked.

"Are you sure we can't bring anything?" Terrell asked.

"No, it's pretty well stocked and Dean and I are going to buy food on the way up."

"I still want to go," Kurt said, pouting towards his husband.

"It's a family wedding, dear. We committed a long time ago. You're going whether you like it or not."

"But we'd have so much more fun at the cabin," Kurt said, looking lustily towards Dean.

"It's not summer camp, it's a cabin," Tony said. "Everyone has their own room and they all have locks on the doors."

"Well, if we're ever invited, which seems increasingly unlikely," Bill said, looking at Tony but nodding towards his husband, "You might want to consider putting a pad lock on the *outside* of our door."

"Oh stop it, we'll be invited up next time, won't we Tony?" Kurt asked.

"I wish you guys could come this trip. I think it would be a lot of fun," Tony said. "I'd forgotten what it was like to have a large circle of friends to just hang out with. It's pretty nice."

"That's sweet," Erik said. "A toast! To old friends and new friends!"

A chorus of cheers went up and for just a moment, everyone forgot the problems in their lives and just enjoyed themselves.

CHAPTER 26

For the first time in a long time, Dean actually felt relaxed. They had all arrived at Tony's cabin on Friday night. *Cabin* was a bit of an understatement, considering the fact that it was a four bedroom log house with a huge family room and a kitchen to die for. It was cold and raining when they arrived, so Tony lit a fire. Bottles of wine were opened, munchies were made, and everyone spent the night laughing and talking until almost two in the morning. There was no drama, no sexual undercurrents between the couples, and no hidden agendas from anyone. It was heaven.

On Saturday morning, Moose and Peter practically had to tie Dean to a dining room chair so that they could make everyone breakfast. After cleaning up, they drove into Saugatuck and spent a leisurely afternoon shopping, with intermittent stops at various bars. Dean picked up a number of items for dinner and, much to Tony's relief, didn't drink all that much.

The truth was he didn't feel like drinking. He wasn't sure if it was the fact that he was so relaxed or the fact that there was no tension between anyone, but he found that he was just enjoying being with his friends.

Dean had decided to prepare a cassoulet with fresh baked bread for dinner Saturday night. He kicked everyone out of the kitchen in order to get the complicated meal prepared. Erik and Terrell went to take a nap, while Moose and Peter went for a walk along the lake. Dean was lost in his preparations when Tony came up behind him and hugged the man that he was falling in love with more every day.

"You seem happy," Tony said.

"That obvious, eh? It's wonderful out here, Tony. I can't believe we're only a couple of hours away from Chicago. I feel like I can breathe here."

"Yeah, when I bought this place, I felt the same way. I need to get up here more. Now that I see how much you like it, we'll definitely have to come back."

"Come back? What makes you think I'm leaving?"

"Well, come Monday morning, reality beckons."

"Reality is highly overrated," Dean said, with a bit of melancholy in his voice.

"I know things have been stressful for you lately, but you know, your life might be a bit easier if you leaned on someone. Hint. Hint."

"I have as much a chance leaning on someone as you do being subtle," Dean said, trying to laugh the subject off.

Tony nuzzled Dean's neck and pulled him close. At times like this, his passion for Dean was only eclipsed by his need to protect him.

"Part of loving you means being there for you. I know that you don't think you need that, but I think you do. Just remember that I'm here for you."

* * * * *

"And what did you say?" Lonny asked an hour or so later. Everyone was napping at this point. Dinner needed just a few small touches, otherwise, it was ready to go. So Dean took a moment to check in on Lonny.

"I said 'thanks'," Dean replied, sheepishly. "That's when he went to take a nap. I think I might have hurt his feelings."

"Oh, you think?"

"Don't start, Lonny, I don't need it right now. See, this is the problem. I was having a great weekend, and everything was going fine, and then he had to drop the love bomb again."

"God, I can't believe how selfish he is," Lonny deadpanned. "How inconsiderate can one man be?"

"You know, if I didn't know you better, I would say that you were directing that comment at me."

"Oh, really? You freakin' think?"

"Instead of getting pissy with me, you might want to take a step back and consider the bigger problem here."

"Which is?"

"He's everything I've ever wanted, and yet, I can't bring myself to tell him that I love him. If I can't tell him, who will I be able to tell? I think I might be seriously messed up."

"You think?" Lonny repeated. "Okay, that was the last one. There is a big difference between telling him you love him and being in love with him. One is a problem with your head; the other is a problem with your heart. I've known you a long time, DeeDee, and there's nothing wrong with your heart."

"Nice. So you're saying I'm crazy."

"Honey, we've all known you're a bit crazy for some time now. It don't make you bad people, as they say here in the South."

"You're such a bitch. I'd be offended if I didn't know that it was a little bit true," Dean said, ruefully.

"A little bit?"

"Don't push it, asswipe."

"See, how could anyone not fall in love with that mouth."

"It's a mystery to me. So what is your advice, since you know me so well?"

"Therapy. Lot's of it."

It took Dean a second to realize that he wasn't joking. "Wow. I thought you were going to just tell me to get over myself and tell him that I love him."

"Do you love him?"

"I don't know. Honestly, I'm not even sure that I know what love is supposed to feel like anymore."

"Again, therapy. Honey, you weren't always like this. Even after your Mom died, you were still open to loving someone. Something has happened in the last few years, and I'll be damned if I know what it is."

"It sounds stupid, but I think it was all the travel. All those years of spending night after night alone in a hotel. Having a trick here and there, but never enough time to really get involved with anyone. Truth is, part of me was relieved that I didn't have to deal with all of the emotions that come with dating and romance. I had my friends and that was enough."

"And now?" Lonny asked, surprised by the turn the conversation had taken. Surprised even more that Dean was actually being honest with himself.

"Now? That's the question I suppose. I just don't know if I have it in me anymore. I know what I should feel, and there are times when I'm with Tony that I do feel something amazing for him. But then I pull back."

"Look, I'm not saying you should tell him that you love him just for the sake of saying it, but you need to figure out what is going on in your head. If not for you, then for him."

"I know, I know. Listen, I hear someone shuffling around. I think the bears are waking from hibernation, I should get dinner ready. Nothing crankier than hungry bears."

"Okay, but think about what I said."

"I have been, believe me. I love you Lonny."

"See how easy that was?" Lonny teased, before hanging up.

* * * * *

Later, after dinner, dessert, and a really bad piece of gay cinema, everyone went out to the hot tub.

"Wow. Six naked men in a hot tub for ten minutes and no one has been groped yet. That must be some kind of record," Moose said, as he sipped his champagne.

"Who said no one was being groped?" Dean asked innocently, his right hand resting in Tony's lap.

"Well, no one who shouldn't be groped by those without the express permission to be groped by the gropee," Tony said, in his best legalese.

"Kurt's not here," Peter said. "So I think we're all relatively safe."

"I hate to say it, but there is a different vibe when they're not around," Moose said.

"I wouldn't be surprised if we started seeing a lot less of them," Terrell said.

"What do you mean?" Dean asked, drawing a glance from Tony.

"Nothing. Forget I said it."

"Oh, hell no," Moose said. "Spill it."

"It's nothing, honestly," Terrell said. He was doing his best to backtrack because he suddenly realized that what was meant to be said out of concern was about to turn into gossip. "It's nothing I've heard or anything. It's just a feeling. I think Bill has had enough. I think he might be ready to tell Kurt that they need to make some changes."

"It's about damn time," Peter said. "Now Dean can roam the streets freely and without fear."

"Stop it, guys. Kurt is harmless and I'm sure things are fine with him and Bill," Dean said.

There was an awkward silence as everyone realized that there had been a shift in the mood. It was one thing to joke about each other, but the sudden realization that two of their own might be in trouble had a sobering effect.

Moose, as usual, couldn't take it. "So, does anyone else have bubbles going up their ass? I kinda like it!"

CHAPTER 27

Dean sprinted up the escalator of the Sears Tower to the second level to find Moose waiting for him outside of Mrs. Levy's delicatessen. He was tapping his watch as Dean approached.

"Sorry! I was trying to get out of there but it has been a very bad day," Dean said.

"I was just giving you shit, baby, don't worry about."

"No, it's not fair to make you wait," Dean said, as he ushered Moose into the restaurant. "Everything seems so crazy lately. I hate it."

"Honey, you seriously have to relax. You were five minutes late. It's not a big deal."

After they were seated, Dean took a few deep breaths while he perused the menu. He knew Moose was right, but still, he hated the fact that he kept him waiting. He just felt so out of sorts. The waiter came and went, and Dean slowly regained his composure.

Moose studied Dean and didn't like what he saw because he knew that for someone who prided himself on always being in control, he seemed to be anything but at the moment. Dean had been fine over the weekend in Saugatuck, but now he seemed distressed.

"Thanks again for the weekend, we had a great time," Moose said, trying to move Dean back to more pleasant thoughts.

"Thank Tony, not me. It's his cabin. I was just along for the ride."

"What does that mean?"

"It means what it means. It's Tony's cabin. He invited you. You were his guest. You should be thanking him, not me."

"Um, okay. Care to tell me why you're being so weird?"

"I just don't want to take credit for something that isn't mine. Yes, we had a great time. Yes, the cabin is beautiful. But it's not like I had anything to do with it. I was a guest – just like you."

"We have the strangest lunches sometimes," Moose said. He stared at Dean and wondered if he would ever understand what was going on inside his head.

"I just don't want it to seem like I'm freeloading," Dean said. "I'm sure you guys must be thinking that I've really bagged a rich one this time."

"Where on earth are you getting that? No one thinks that, Dean. No one except you apparently."

"Forget I said it, its not important. It was nice spending time with you guys. I know that lately we haven't been doing that as much as we should."

"Again, what are you talking about? We're constantly together."

"Not really. Not as much as we used to be. It's so hard to balance work and friends and dating. I'm starting to feel that I'm not giving enough to any of them."

"Honey, that's the nature of life. Things ebb and flow. Everyone understands that you're dating someone and we're all happy for you. We still see plenty of you. You don't need to worry about that."

"I don't know. I was talking to Kurt and he said that everyone feels like I've disappeared."

"Oh Christ, I should have guessed," Moose said angrily. "You know, Kurt may not be the most objective person to have an opinion about your relationship or anything else that is going on in your life, for that matter. And for him to say *everyone* feels that way is just a fucking lie."

"I'm aware that he might have an ulterior motive, but he also has a point. There have been a lot of things you guys have done over the past few months that I haven't been able to do because I've been spending time with Tony."

"And thank God for that. Do you understand that your friends are supposed to be happy for you when you find someone that you care about? That they aren't supposed to make you feel guilty about it? Fuck Kurt and what he says."

"Stop yelling at me! I'm having a hard time right now. You know, when we were at the cabin, everything was great. Now it's back to reality and its one damn thing after another. I feel like everything is just fucked up."

"I'm not yelling at you, I'm yelling at Kurt. You just happen to be here. You know, letting your life get a little out of control isn't the worst thing in the world. Actually, for most of us, that's the way it is. Life is messy, relationships are hard. It's okay to get overwhelmed by it all. It just means that you're human."

"I know, and you're probably right. I'm just really stressed out. This weekend isn't going to help."

"When do you and Tony fly down?"

"We're leaving Friday afternoon," Dean said, his voice tinged with sadness. "I'm so afraid that every time I see Lonny it's going to be the last time."

"I know, honey. We were chatting with him last night and I could tell how tired he was. You probably don't want to hear this but when it's over, it will be for the best."

"I suppose. I know how hard this has been for him. I truly do. There are times when I think 'just let it be over already.'

Then, after I get over the guilt of thinking that, I realize that once he's gone, I've got nothing left."

"What do you mean?" Moose asked.

"Don't get me wrong, I'm not saying that you and Peter and everyone else don't mean the world to me, but Lonny is the only link to my childhood, my past. He's all I have left of that part of my life. When he's gone, it's gone. I'm just this person drifting through life."

"That's not true. You've got your friends and you've got Tony."

"I know I have you guys, and like I said, you all mean a lot to me. Still, I feel like I'm becoming an orphan all over again."

"Actually, Dean, what I said was that you have us and you have Tony. You seemed to have missed that part."

"I heard you. But let's be honest – given my track record, how long do you really think Tony is going to be around?" Dean asked. He couldn't bring himself to look at Moose because he didn't want to deal with the judgment that he knew he would see there.

"Wow, you're unbelievable. You're starting it already."

"What are you talking about?"

"The infamous Dean retreat. You're already thinking of how to end things with Tony."

"No, I'm not. You guys seem to think that everything is just perfect for me and Tony, and I'll be honest, for the most part, things are great. But there are things that you don't know about us that concern me."

"You mean like the fact that you can't tell him you love him?" Moose asked.

Dean was stunned. "Wow, you guys really have become close. Did he tell you anything else about us? Positions? Frequency? Any other things about me that he's disappointed in?"

"Rein it in, princess paranoid. Let's not forget that Peter and I have been friends with Tony for a lot of years."

"I don't care, he had no right to talk about me."

"I'm going to put aside for the moment how hurt I am that *you* didn't bother to tell me. I love you, Dean. Next to Lonny, there isn't anyone in this world who knows you better than me. So here's a little newsflash. You are in love with Tony. And I don't think the problem is that you can't feel it – I think the problem is that you feel it with every fiber of your being and it scares the shit out of you."

"Wonderful, you're a shrink now too."

"No, I'm just one of your best damn friends in the world. And I happen to be someone who's madly in love with the man of his dreams, so I know what it feels like and I know what it looks like and you reek of it whether you like it or not."

"Can we change the subject please?"

Surprisingly, Moose agreed. He was right on one score – they did have the oddest lunches. Still, Dean spent the rest of the meal half listening to Moose and half pondering what he had said. No matter how he sliced it, it wasn't good. Either he was incapable of love or terrified by it. Maybe Lonny was right and he needed to start seeing a therapist. How could he be so happy one minute, like he was in Saugatuck, and be so freaked out and miserable the next? It seemed as if he was always thinking that things would get better after the next big thing – after the next board meeting, after the next trip, after Lonny passed away, after...everything. Happiness always seemed to be just over the horizon and always outside of his reach.

CHAPTER 28

Dean and Tony were sitting outside basking in the late afternoon sun on Cordova Street in St. Augustine's tourist district. The humidity that so often suffocated Florida had taken the day off and they relished the feeling of the cool breeze drifting through the city. After their plane had landed, Dean called Lonny's mother to find out what the plans for the day were. She told him that it was pretty low key and that Lonny was taking a nap and would probably be out for a few hours.

Deciding that real live pictures were worth more than a thousand words, Dean took Tony on a tour of his childhood, trailer park and all.

As they sipped their cappuccinos in a café that was roughly five miles from where Dean grew up, there was a silence between them that Tony didn't like. He had felt Dean withdrawing into himself, and this trip was only making matters worse. But it was also explaining a lot.

"You're awfully quiet," Tony said.

"I was just thinking about my Mom. I think about her a lot

whenever I'm down here."

"You don't talk much about her. I know we've talked about your Dad a few times, but whenever I bring up your Mom, you change the subject."

"Hey, look, that cloud is shaped like a bunny rabbit."

"Funny man. I'm serious. When did your Mom pass away?"

Dean was quiet for a long time. There was a look of such sadness on his face that Tony was suddenly sorry he had asked the question.

"She died my freshman year in college. Well, *died* isn't really the right word. She killed herself."

"God, Dean, I'm sorry."

"It's not your fault. I've been trying to get to the point where I don't think it's my fault, either, but I haven't been that successful."

"What do you mean? How could it be your fault?"

"I don't know. I sometimes feel like I abandoned her. After my Dad died, I was really all she had. Once I went away to college, the wheels came off pretty fast. I left for Florida State in late August, and she died in November. Right there in the trailer."

"I don't know what to say," Tony said.

"Not much to say, I suppose. I sometimes think I should have done more. Called More. Tried to come home on weekends. Asked her to move to Tallahassee. I don't know."

"Honey, it's not your fault. You have to know that."

"Have you ever known anyone who committed suicide? Believe me, sometimes you can't help but think it's your fault. It's bad enough when someone you love dies and you're there with them, holding their hand as they leave. It's so much worse when you're away from them. You wonder what their last moments must have been like. Then, when its suicide, you end up piling guilt on top of everything else you're feeling. When I think of her in that shabby room, sitting on that bed, thinking that there was nothing else to do but swallow those pills, it breaks my heart. If she would have just picked up the phone and called me, I would have dropped everything and found a way to help her."

Dean had sometimes hinted about how difficult his life had been, and Tony had picked up pieces of it over the months that they had been together. But it wasn't until this trip and this conversation that he was finally able to put it all together and see how hard things had been for him. Tony thought about his own life, and the support of his family, his comfortable upbringing, his long relationship with Steve. When he compared that to Dean's experiences, he suddenly began to understand why it might be difficult for Dean to allow himself to open up to him. It just made him love Dean all the more.

"This is probably the last time I'll ever see this place," Dean said suddenly. "I mean, I'll come back down for the funeral. But the city, the trailer, my school, I'll never see them again. I honestly never want to see any of it again, and yet it still makes me sad. It must be nice, for you, to go home and be surrounded by everything you had when you were growing up - to feel that sense of history, of continuity."

"I guess. I don't really think about it like that. Chicago is my home now, not Boston. When I'm at my parents' house, there's so much family stuff going on and so many people to see that I don't have time to dwell on the past."

Dean grunted a response, but other than that, was quiet.

"What's going on, Dean?"

"I wish I knew. I feel like things are coming apart for me. I thought as it got closer to the end for Lonny I would gain some sort of acceptance or peace about it. But the truth is, with every passing day, it gets worse. And the pathetic part is, its getting bad not because of Lonny, but because of what Lonny dying means for me. Its selfish and weird and I don't know what to do about it."

"It's not weird at all. Take it from someone who's been there, the death of someone you love is in some ways inevitably a selfish experience. You worry about the person you're losing, but I think you end up worrying even more about what is going to happen to you when they are gone."

Dean nodded in agreement, but again, said nothing. Tony knew the battle that was being raged within him, because he'd been through it himself. He only survived Steve's death because of the support of his family and friends. He knew that Dean had no family, but he had a great many friends, and he had Tony. He couldn't understand why Dean was determined to push people away, just when he needed them the most.

"You're not alone, Dean," Tony said, as he took Dean's hand. "You know I'm crazy in love with you, and I'll always be here for you. I know you don't know where we're heading, and if things don't work out for us, you still have your friends. I wish you could see how many people care for you – and how much they care for you."

"We should get going to Lonny's house," Dean said, as he removed Tony's hand and stood up. "Besides, we're in a red state, you could get us shot holding my hand."

Tony stood and followed Dean up the cobblestone street back towards their car. He knew Dean was hurting, and he knew Dean was pulling away, but he was also beginning to wonder how long he would be able to put up with the distance between them. He loved Dean, but he wasn't without pride either. If Dean wanted to push him away, it wouldn't be impossible.

* * * * *

Lonny was awake and somewhat rejuvenated by the time they got to the house. The entire Turnow family had shown up for dinner and it was a blast. The arrival of so many loved ones seemed to give Lonny renewed strength. He bombarded Tony with questions about his life and his past and how he felt about Dean. Tony laughed and went along with it all until Lonny finally announced that he approved. Dean spent most of the afternoon and evening watching, smiling and enjoying the feeling of family that he always felt at the Turnow home.

But through all of the stories and jokes and memories, there was an underlying sense of sadness. Every now and then, when it seemed that no one else was looking, Dean would catch Donny or Connie looking at their son with such heartbreak that Dean was barely able to hold it together. At one point, during a story that his sister was telling about Lonny, his mother was laughing so hard that she started crying. Then she started crying for real, but excused herself before anyone could take notice. Everyone noticed, of course.

Later, Dean, Tony and Lonny sat on the back porch in the candlelight and enjoyed the cool night air. As much as Dean hated the memories of his past and his life in Florida, when the sun went down and the sounds of the night took over, there was a serenity that he always appreciated. Peace was always in such short supply for him that he relished it whenever he could experience it.

"So my mother has ordered me to tell you again that she fully expects you to be on her doorstep every Christmas for years to come," Lonny said to Dean. "Unless of course, you're going to be spending your holidays with Tony."

Dean started to protest both the assumption that he would be with Tony next winter and that Lonny wouldn't be around for Christmas, but Lonny cut him off.

"Her words, not mine. Take it up with Big Mama if you have a problem."

"I'll be here at Christmas, with you and your family, just like always." Dean said.

Tony sat quietly. He knew that it was a discussion that he really shouldn't be a part of, for many reasons. He had the feeling that if there weren't a thing in the world wrong with Lonny he would still be in the position that he was in with Dean, which was slowly watching him slip away from him.

"I'm going to get some more tea," Dean said, grabbing Lonny and Tony's glasses as he went into the kitchen. It was getting to be too much, he thought. He could hear Tony and

Lonny talking outside as he refilled their glasses. He couldn't quite make out what they were saying, but he was sure they were talking about him. How difficult he was. How hard it must be for Tony to deal with him. Dean shook his head. There was no point in thinking about it.

"Got demons in your head?" Lonny's father asked from the doorway, startling Dean.

"No, no. Just...yeah," Dean finally said.

"I can understand that. Been doing a lot of that myself lately," Donny said as he grabbed a slice of cheesecake from the refrigerator. "Don't tell Lonny's mama about this."

Dean made the symbol for sealed lips and started cleaning up the mess he'd made when Donny startled him.

"You're friend seems really nice," Donny said. "The grandkids loved him. You boys happy?"

Dean looked at Donny and started laughing.

"What's so funny?"

"Nothing. Everything. When I was eleven, twelve years old and tearing around here with Lonny, did you ever imagine the day would come when you would be asking me how my boyfriend and I were getting along?"

"No, I can't say as I did. Things change I suppose," Donny said, laughing softly. From his spot in the kitchen, he could see Lonny engrossed in conversation with Tony. "There are a lot of things I never would have imagined would happen when you two were boys."

Dean could see the pain in his eyes and for just a moment thought of his own father. Sons losing fathers. Fathers losing sons. Everyone losing everyone. What was the point of so much love if it was just going to be taken away from you?

"I guess I'm not so hungry after all," Donny said, placing the cheesecake back in the refrigerator. Much to Dean's surprise, he came over and kissed him on the cheek. "Sleep well, son."

When Donny was safely out of sight, Dean lost it. The crying jag came on so hard and so fast that there was no way to stop it, even if he wanted to. He grabbed a towel from the counter and buried his face in it so that no one would hear. The last thing he needed, he thought, was anyone seeing him like this. He was wrong, of course, but he was who he was. He took a few deep breaths, wiped away the tears, pushed away the pain and pulled himself together. The night was still relatively young and Lonny was feeling well, so he went out to spend whatever time he could with his friend. His pain could wait.

CHAPTER 29

On Saturday night, a few days after they returned from Florida, Dean and Tony met everyone out at Charlie's. Dean had been going non-stop since they got back and he definitely felt the need for a night on the town. There had been times over the last few weeks, when he had a few spare moments to think, that he realized things were spinning out of control. The rational part of his mind tried to tell him to slow down but the part of him that needed to be all things to all people just couldn't see a break in the relentless stream of obligations.

Tony had been trying to get him to take it easy, but the more he pushed, the more Dean resisted. It almost seemed like he was trying to drive himself into exhaustion. He and Tony had gotten into an argument earlier in the day because Tony thought the last thing they needed was a night spent in a bar.

"Can't we just stay in and be with each other and relax?" Tony had asked.

"I haven't seen the guys in over a week, and I want to spend some time with them. I miss them. My friends are very important to me, you know that."

"You know I don't like the bars that much."

"Then don't go, Tony. We don't have to spend every minute together," Dean snapped.

"What the hell is that supposed to mean?"

"We spent last night together. I have no doubt that we'll spend tomorrow together. Tonight, I want to see my friends. It would be great if you were there, but if you don't want to come, then don't come."

In the end, Tony had agreed to go, if for no other reason than he couldn't stop worrying about Dean. It was getting harder and harder to figure out what was going on between them. He loved Dean desperately, but he was starting to think that it wasn't enough. Of all of the things that seemed to take up Dean's time – work, Lonny, his friends – Tony was starting to wonder if Dean thought that maybe he would be the easiest to get rid of.

An hour after they arrived, Dean was well into his fourth drink and far too cozy with Kurt for anyone's comfort.

"You might want to unhitch yourself from Kurt's pelvis and head over by your husband," Moose whispered.

"He's not my husband," Dean said.

"Whatever. Husband. Boyfriend. Man toy. I don't care what you call him, but I think you're pissing him off."

"Oh, leave him alone," Kurt said, wrapping his arms around Dean's waist. "We're all having a good time. No harm, no foul. You don't see Bill getting all pouty."

"I think I would actually have to care in order to be pouty," Bill said.

"See?" Kurt said, oblivious to the meaning behind the words, having long since stopped listening to what his husband had to say.

Tony, however, had not stopped caring. He had also seen enough of Dean's antics for one night. Walking up to Dean and Kurt, he inserted himself between them and ordered another bottle of water from the bartender.

"Would you like some water?" he asked Dean.

"No, sweetie, I'm good," Dean said, raising his glass in a toast and giggling.

"I don't think I've ever noticed your ass before," Kurt said loudly, as he admired Tony's backside. He gave it a good slap, and for just a moment, everyone held their breath. But Tony didn't take the bait. Not too much, anyway.

"That's odd, because I've noticed you were an ass from the moment I met you," Tony said, drawing laughter from everyone, especially Bill.

"Now see, I was trying to give you a compliment and you have to get all bitchy on me. You know what? Maybe the four of us should just go home together. You can fuck this one," Kurt said, jerking a thumb towards Bill, "And I can take another crack at Dean. Maybe that will help you lighten up a bit."

Kurt was doing his best to get a rise out of Tony, but before he could react, Bill had set his glass down and started heading for the door, without a word to anyone.

"I think your soon-to-be ex-husband just left," Tony said, taking no satisfaction in it.

Even Kurt realized that he might have gone too far, but still tried to hide his sudden concern with a false sense of bravado.

"Oh well, I guess I better go catch him. We'll be back," he said, as he shrugged on his coat.

"We won't be here," Tony said, looking at Dean.

"Well then, I better give you a good night kiss," Dean said, as he kissed Kurt deeply. Kurt was taken aback as he realized that things were way out of control, even for him. He left the group and went out into the night to find Bill.

"Well, this has been fun, but I think we're going to head home too," Moose said, before whispering in Dean's ear, "You're seriously fucking up."

Dean just raised his glass in another salute as he watched Moose and Peter leave.

"Well, I guess we might as well leave, too. Lord knows you

didn't want to be here in the first place," Dean said.

They walked in silence back to Dean's apartment. The brisk night air was sobering Dean up, but only slightly. More than once Tony had to reach out to keep Dean from tripping. Tony helped him inside and then left him standing there. By the time Dean made it to the bedroom, Tony was brushing his teeth and almost ready to turn in.

"So, are you ignoring me now?" Dean asked, as he unsteadily began to take off his clothes.

"No, but I don't want to have this conversation with you when you're drunk."

"This conversation?"

"Not now, Dean. Seriously."

"Whatever," Dean said, as he threw his shoes across the room. "Heaven forbid we don't do things your way."

"You want to get into this? Fine. If you ever, and I mean *ever*, treat me that way again in front of our friends, I will walk. I know you're going through a lot of shit, and I've put up with a lot from you because of that, but here's where I draw the line. You and I are not Kurt and Bill. You're with me, and I'm with you, and don't you ever disrespect me or our relationship like that again."

"Oh give me a fucking break. I wasn't disrespecting anything. We were just having fun. And you'll have to excuse me, but the way things are going with my life, I'll take my fun where I can find it."

"No matter who gets hurt?"

"Who got hurt, Tony? Seriously, who?"

"Are you so fucked up that you didn't see Bill walk out on everyone? Did you think he was having fun? More importantly, did it seem like I was having fun?"

"Well you need to lighten up," Dean said, but without much conviction. "Look, I'm sorry, okay? I was just blowing off some steam and clearly drinking too much. Things just got out of hand."

"Do you want to be with me, Dean?"

"What?" Dean was surprised by the bluntness of the question.

"Do you want to be with me? I'm not asking you if you're in love with me, but I need to know that there is something here worth fighting for. If there's some sort of future between us, I'll move heaven and earth to make it happen, but if you really don't give a shit, then have the decency to let me know so we can both move on."

"Jesus, Tony, why does everything have to be life or death with you? Yes I care for you. Yes, I want us to continue seeing each other. But we've only been dating a few months – is it okay that we don't pin our entire lives on the outcome of this relationship?"

"But that's what relationships are, Dean. The good ones, anyway. You hope that the person you're sleeping next to now is the person that you want to wake up with tomorrow. And the day after that. Forever. It's the thing everyone hopes for."

"Yeah, for about four or five years, then they start fucking other people to spice things up," Dean said, bitterly.

"Some people, maybe. Not me. With me, it's all or nothing."

"And can you understand that I can't make all or nothing, lifetime decisions right now? I'm having trouble getting through the day and you want me to figure out the rest of my life."

"No. I just want to know that you care about me. Even a little. That would be enough for me right now."

"I told you that I care for you."

"Yeah, you told me. I guess that will have to do."

"What the hell do you want from me?" Dean said, his frustration boiling over.

"Nothing. You know, Dean, you either get it or you don't. Maybe tomorrow, when you're sober, you'll understand what I'm trying to say. Let's just go to bed."

It was an abrupt end to the conversation. Dean knew that he should pursue it further, but he also knew that he wasn't going to be able to say the things that Tony wanted to hear, so why put them both through it? Moments later, Dean turned out the lights and crawled into bed next to Tony. For the first time since their first time, there was no good night kiss. No *good night* for that matter. Just a cold silence that filled room. The night wore on, but sleep didn't come for Dean.

CHAPTER 30

Dean was at his desk at his usual time on Monday morning and calmer than he had been in weeks. Unfortunately, it wasn't a good calm. He felt numb. It was as if his mind had finally decided that it couldn't take any more input and needed to shut down for awhile.

Tony had spent Sunday at his office, which almost never happened, so Dean spent Sunday morning trying to get some things done around the apartment. He waited for Tony to call, but he never did. He knew that he had crossed the line on Saturday night. He also knew that he should have called Tony and apologized. Instead, he went to bed Sunday wondering if he had messed things up beyond any hope of fixing them. He also wondered if he really cared. After all, the little voice in his head said, if Tony was done with their relationship, then that was Dean's way out. One less thing to worry about. If only that little voice could convince the rest of him.

"So why haven't you called him?" Lonny asked when he called on Monday morning.

"What's the point?"

"The point is you fucked up and you need to apologize."

"I don't really need this right now, Lonny."

"Of course you do, otherwise, you wouldn't have bothered to tell me what was going on."

"You suck," Dean said, acknowledging the truth.

"Yes, but don't change the subject. Call him."

"I know, I know. Why is it always so hard for me to make things work?"

"I could rattle off the list of reasons, but we've been through them all before. The truth is, I just don't think you know how to be happy, Dean."

"Well, that's a new one. Thanks."

"I don't really know what else to say. Everything you've told me about Tony, everything I saw in Tony, is everything that you've ever wanted in a guy. You said it yourself. More importantly, there were times when you two were down here, that I could tell how much you loved him. It's obvious to everyone but you."

"So you're saying I should call him?"

Lonny laughed. "Yeah, sweetie, I think that might be a good idea."

"What am I going to do without you?" Dean asked, not for the first time.

"How about we focus on the things that you can control, rather than the things that are out of your hands?"

"I hate it when you're right."

"Really? One would think you'd be used to it by now."

"Blow me. I'll talk to you later. Thanks, Lonny."

"Be good sweetie, I love you."

"Love you too," Dean said, as he hung up the phone, then, immediately picked it back up. "No rest for the wicked."

* * * * *

"So what did Tony say?" Moose asked later.

"Not much, really. I apologized and he said that we should

just forget about it. Plus, he didn't really feel like having that particular conversation on the phone."

"I can understand that," Moose said. They had planned to meet for lunch, but Dean wasn't really hungry, so they went for a walk along the river front. They stopped at the Merc along the way and Moose picked up a hot dog, which he was diligently trying to not get all over his shirt as they walked. They finally stopped and leaned against a rail overlooking the water.

"It's just all so stupid," Dean said.

"What?"

"Relationships. You and Peter have this great relationship, and yet you guys fool around with others. Kurt and Bill fool around. I know for a fact that even Erik and Terrell have had at least one three-way. Everyone ends up doing it, so why is it such a big deal at the beginning of a relationship? Why does a little flirting cause such drama, when a few years down the road almost all relationships end up being open anyway?"

"Is that what you want? An open relationship?"

"No, it's just the hypocrisy that bothers me."

"Oh, spare me, please," Moose said.

"What? I'm serious."

"No, you're just looking for reasons for this thing with Tony not to work. You don't want an open relationship. Tony doesn't want an open relationship. Stop worrying about what other people are doing and worry about yourself and what's right for you. Just get over yourself already."

"You know, my friends really are thinking very highly of me today," Dean said.

"We think the world of you. If we didn't care so much, we wouldn't even bother. I just don't want to see you mess this thing up."

"Am I such a loser if I don't have Tony in my life? Do you guys really think so little of me?"

"Again, we love you. You know that. But we also know you. I know that Tony is the best thing that has happened to you in a long, long time. If things don't work out, I'm sure you'll go on and have a nice life without him. The question is, wouldn't your life be better with him?"

"Who knows?"

"You're impossible," Moose said, as he finished off his hot dog. "So what's next?"

"Tony and I are going to have a date-date on Saturday night. Just the two of us. Dinner and a DVD or something like that. We'll see how things go."

"What does that mean?"

"It means we'll see how it goes. I'm starting to wonder if things can be fixed between us."

"Dean, it was one fight. You make up and you move on."

"If that's what both of us want."

"It's pretty obvious that's what Tony wants. What do you want? I mean, seriously Dean, have you ever stopped and tried to figure out what it is you want?"

"God no, then I might have to actually do something about it," Dean joked, but they both knew he was telling the truth.

They began walking back towards their offices on the other side of the Loop.

"Lonny sounded good this morning," Dean said, trying to find a subject that they wouldn't fight about.

"Yeah. I spoke with him this morning too. He sounded a little stronger. He's worried about you, though."

"Everyone's worried about me. I'm a big boy. I'll get through, I always do."

"There's so much more to life than just getting through it. I think if you just let yourself, things could be really amazing for you."

"I am who I am, Moose. I know that I may not be the greatest person in the world, but considering where I came from, and what I've been through, I think I've done pretty well. I hope, as my friend, you can at least appreciate that."

"I do, honey, I do. But I hope you understand that as your friend, I'm going to continue to hope for more for you - and be a royal pain in the ass until you do what I say."

They walked the rest of the way in silence. For some strange reason, Dean felt better. Maybe his circle of friends was shrinking, but the one's he had left were pretty great. Still, Moose's words echoed in his ears. With so much more to life than what Dean had, why couldn't he allow himself to experience it?

CHAPTER 31

Whatever had created the disturbing sense of calm that Dean had felt at the beginning of the week was long gone by Saturday night. The dual pressures of work and Lonny's illness had exploded over the course of the week and Dean's schizophrenic life took another downturn.

On Tuesday morning, Lonny had again been hospitalized with a high fever and stayed there until Thursday night. Meanwhile, Dean had no less than fifteen meetings during the week and each one seemed to present a bigger problem to solve or another political situation to deal with. In between meetings he was trying to keep track of Lonny's progress with frequent phone calls to his mother. His incessant questioning and frantic tone proved to be too much for Connie, and by Thursday morning, Donny had called and told him that Dean was upsetting his wife and that they would contact him when Lonny's condition changed. Tony had also wanted to get together during the week, but Dean just couldn't find the time to do it.

Donny called Dean Thursday night to tell him that Lonny

was home and more or less out of the woods. It was another two days before Lonny felt well enough to call.

"So, DeeDee, how has your week been?" Lonny joked.

"God, it's good to hear your voice. How are you feeling?"

"Eh, you know. It was a bad week, but I'm still here. Mother is less than pleased with you."

"I can imagine. I was a bit dramatic whenever I got her on the phone. How mad is she?"

"She'll be fine. I'm more worried about you. Are you all right?"

"Let's focus on you, that's what I'm worried about. What did the doctor say?"

"Oh, I'm all cured."

"That's not funny, Lonny."

"He said that my system is getting weaker, which caused the fever and that I can expect more breakdowns of one type or another before it's all over."

"How can you be so calm about this?" Dean asked, his heart breaking.

"Because I've accepted it, DeeDee. Everyone seems to have accepted it but you. I mean, you do get it, don't you? I don't have very long."

"Can we please change the subject?"

"Sure, honey, but like it or not, you're going to be dealing with this sooner rather than later."

"Fine, let's make it later."

"Fine. So what are you up to tonight?"

"I'm supposed to have dinner with Tony. I think he's still pissed about what happened at Charlie's," Dean said, clearly not relishing the evening ahead.

"It's just a bump in the road, I'm sure you'll get past it."

"I don't know. Honestly, I don't even know if I care. I don't really have time for this. My life is crazy enough without Tony laying all this bullshit on me."

"Tony is an important part of your life – just as important as all the other parts, if not more so. And let's not forget, this is bullshit of your own making."

"Whatever, I don't want to get into this with you, too. You're the most important thing in my life right now."

"And when I'm gone? Then what, Dean? Do you have any idea how much time I spend worrying about you? I've managed to make peace with every part of my life and everyone I love, except for you. I'm so worried about you."

"Why don't you just worry about yourself," Dean said quietly. "I can take care of myself."

"Listen, my mom is standing in front of me with a look that would make Nurse Ratched proud, so I need to go. Do me a favor?"

"Sure," Dean said, noncommittally.

"Don't do anything rash about Tony. He's a good guy."

"So am I, Lonny. Not that any of my friends seem to think so."

"We all think that, DeeDee. The problem is, you never quite believe us. I have to run. I Love you," Lonny said.

"I love you too, Lonny. I'll talk to you tomorrow."

* * * * *

When Dean arrived at Tony's house a few hours later, he was still a mess. Tony took his jacket and tried to give him a kiss, but Dean just gave him a quick peck on the cheek. Tony could tell that Dean was agitated, and considering his plans for the evening, he didn't want to upset Dean from the moment he walked through the door. As he hung up his jacket, he watched as Dean went straight for the kitchen to make himself a drink.

"How are you feeling?" Tony asked, already knowing the answer.

"Well, according to popular opinion, I'm falling apart," Dean said, as he gulped down half of the vodka and cranberry that he had just made.

"Yeah, I heard. Considering everything you've been going through, that's not so surprising."

"What do you mean you heard?" Dean asked suspiciously, as he topped off his drink with more vodka.

"Nothing, really. I was talking to Moose earlier and he said that you were pretty upset about everything that was going on with Lonny and that work was making you crazy. He wanted to make sure that I provided plenty of TLC this weekend."

"Wonderful. You're talking to my friends about me now. Are you guys going to hold an intervention?"

"It wasn't like that. He was just worried about you. And keep in mind, they're my friends too."

"Well, I'm sure they'd rather be hanging out with you instead of me right now. Look, I'm just stressed out. I mean, fuck, don't you think that I have the right to be? My best friend is dying. Once he's gone, that's it. I'm on my own. Does anyone get that?"

"You've got your friends here, Dean. And you've got me. I'd like to think that counts for something."

"Tony, we've been seeing each other for what – four or five months? Do you know the longest I've been with anyone is a year? A year! What makes you think this is going to last?"

"Hope, I suppose," Tony said.

It occurred to Dean that this was the same conversation that he had with Moose. Maybe Moose and Tony had talked about that, too. Dean just laughed and started to pour himself another drink. Tony grabbed his hand, then grabbed the bottle and set it down on the counter.

"Listen, I want to talk to you about something, and I'd prefer that you be sober when I do," Tony said. He took Dean's hand and led him to the sofa.

"Tony, I can't deal with a heavy conversation right now, I really can't. I've got so much shit going on in my head that if I have to deal with one more thing, I swear I don't know what I'll do."

"That's just it, Dean. I'm the one that you're supposed to be having these conversations with. I'm the one who's here for you and who's supposed to be helping you deal with all of this stuff that you're going through. It just kills me to think that you can't lean on me – especially now."

"Tony, honest to God, I don't know what you want from me."

"I want to know that I'm part of your life. A big part of your life. Right now you seem to be treating me like some kind of nuisance rather than someone who should be one of the most important people in your life. It hurts me to think that you can't trust me."

"If you want to help me, then right now you just need to give me some space. I'm dealing with too much to have to worry about how I'm making you feel."

"Did you understand a word I just said? I'm not asking you to worry about how I feel. I'm telling you that you need to let me help you through this."

"This is who I am, Tony. I'm sorry if I'm not giving you enough or leaning on you enough or doing whatever it is that you think I need to be doing. I've told you before that I've always had to depend on myself. I'm sorry if you're love for me isn't some magic potion that allows me to open up to you in the way that you want me to."

"So what am I to you then?" Tony asked. "If I'm just someone to have on the sidelines, or worse, a burden...I don't want to be that, Dean. I want more than that from you. From us."

"I'm giving you everything I can right now. If that's not enough, then I can't help you. Maybe you should be looking for someone needier."

"You really don't get it do you?"

"Fuck, I guess not! Why don't you explain it to me? Why don't you tell me everything I'm doing wrong and then I'll try to fix myself for you. You'll understand, however, if I take a few minutes every now and then to worry about my best friend, who's dying; my job, which is kicking my ass every day; and my friends, who I don't see nearly as much as I would like."

"Dean, I'm just trying to help you."

"I don't need any help and I'm done with this conversation," Dean said, as he stood up. "I'm sorry. I just can't do this right now. I'm completely maxed out mentally and this isn't helping. I'm just going to go home. We can talk tomorrow."

"No, Dean, we're going to finish this now."

Dean stared at him. This was it then? It was as if he was outside his body watching what was happening and knowing what was coming and not being able to do a damn thing about it. And God help him, he didn't care.

"Okay, fine, we're finished," Dean said.

"I'm serious, Dean."

"So am I. We're finished. Not this conversation – us."

"What?" Tony was stunned.

"I'm sorry, but I can't do this. I'll be the bad guy. You can tell everyone what a dick I am. Do whatever you want. I just can't do this anymore. I've got too much else to worry about," Dean said as he went to get his jacket.

"Just like that? You're going to walk out of here and it's over? Just like that?"

"No, not *just like that*. This may be hard for you to believe, but this is killing me. But I'm tired of feeling like shit because I can't give you what you need."

"You were looking for a way out of this, weren't you?" Tony asked, his disbelief quickly turning to anger. "You came here looking for a way to end this."

"No, actually, I didn't. But to be completely honest, I'm glad it's done. It's kind of a relief," Dean said, even though his heart was breaking. A small part of him wanted to rush into Tony's arms, but as always, he held himself back.

"Goodbye, Dean," Tony said, with a coldness that Dean didn't think he was capable of.

"Tony, look, in a few days, we can talk. I'd like for us to still be friends."

Tony just stared at him. Dean really couldn't believe that it had come to this, and yet, he was being truthful when he said it was a relief. He turned and left, with Tony staring after him. He was barely down the steps when he heard Tony's hand on the door. Dean turned around but instead of seeing the door open, he heard the lock click into place. He turned back around, and started walking down the street. Alone.

CHAPTER 32

I n the days that followed their breakup, Dean managed to avoid everyone, which was no easy feat considering how tight his group of friends were. Letting Tony tell their friends that they had broken up was the coward's way out, but Dean didn't care. As he made his way to the bowling alley on Wednesday night, he still felt horrible over the way it had all gone down. He had been a mess on Sunday, knowing that he had fucked up again with Tony. This time he realized there was no going back. But again, he couldn't help feeling some small sense of relief.

The only person he had broken the news to was Lonny – and his friend let him have it with both barrels.

"What part of 'don't do anything rash' did you not understand?" Lonny had asked on Sunday morning.

"It's not like I planned it. Things just sort of spiraled out of control."

"Really? Or were you looking for a way out?" he asked, echoing what Tony had said.

"No, it just happened. Lonny, I feel bad enough about this

without you giving me grief about it."

"Whatever. I don't give a fuck anymore."

Their conversation had deteriorated from that point, until Lonny had finally hung up on him. They made up the next day, both of them realizing that time was short and arguing was not what either of them needed. He asked Lonny not to mention what happened to anyone because he wanted to avoid a confrontation for as long as he could. When he entered the bowling alley, he immediately saw his friends and went over to face the music.

There were the usual hugs and kisses as Dean unpacked his bag. As he was putting on his bowling shoes he realized that he wasn't the only one who had been ducking his friends. They didn't know about the breakup.

"Listen up everybody," Moose said, as he came back from polishing off a spare, "The weather is supposed to be gorgeous this weekend so we're thinking of having a pre-summer barbeque on Sunday afternoon, if everyone's free."

There were nods of agreement and small talk about the burst of warm weather Chicago was enjoying. Dean remained quiet and grabbed his ball. He wanted to run but knew that there was nowhere to go. He was wiping his ball down when Peter stopped him.

"Hey, space cadet, I don't know how many wieners to buy if I don't know who's coming. Are you guys free on Sunday?"

"I'm free. I don't know about Tony," Dean said, putting off the inevitable for a few more seconds.

"Well, we'll just ask him when he comes in later. He will be coming in later, right Dean?" Moose asked, aware that something was wrong.

"That seems unlikely," Dean said, as he put down the ball and faced his friends. "We broke up this weekend."

Everyone sat in stunned silence as Dean stared at them. The team that they were playing realized what was going on and started talking amongst themselves, trying to avoid the drama that was unfolding next to them.

"You're joking," Moose finally said.

"No, Moose, I'm not joking. We had a fight, it got out of control and we broke up."

"*We* broke up, or you broke up with him?"

"Fine. Yes. I broke up with him. This isn't the first time that I've broken up with someone so take your jaws off the floor." Dean could feel his face flush.

"Well, whatever you did, you need to apologize and get back together with him."

"Thank you so much for assuming that it was something I did that led me to break up with him. It's nice to know how you really feel."

"What happened?" Bill asked, unhappy at the thought of a suddenly single Dean.

"Honestly, I'm surprised that you guys don't already know. I can't believe that he didn't hop on the phone to his buddies here," Dean said, nodding towards Moose and Peter, "And tell them what a terrible prick I am."

"Well, he probably doesn't want anything to do with us now," Moose said.

"I'm so sorry, but if you like, you can have him in the divorce. Does that make you feel better?"

"Dean, what happened?" Peter asked.

"We had a fight. It was a stupid fight that got out of hand and I ended up breaking things off with him. Look, don't get me wrong. I care about Tony deeply, but he just wants more from me than I can give right now. There's only so much of me to go around and something had to give. I wish I were a better person or a stronger person or whatever, but I'm not. Now I know that for whatever reason, you guys are disappointed, but believe me when I say, this is for the best right now."

"Nice speech," Moose said derisively. "How many times did you have to repeat it in front of the mirror before you actually believed it?"

"I know that I'm back to just being a lonely, pathetic single person, but do you think you could find it in your big married heart to cut me some fucking slack?"

"Oh, don't give me that shit, Dean. The pity party doesn't work with me. I don't care if you're single or married. I do care, however, if you keep fucking up your life," Moose said.

Dean was just about to unload on Moose when Kurt intervened. "Leave him alone. It's none of our business. Dean is our friend and we'll support him whatever he does."

"Oh give me a fucking break!" Moose exclaimed.

"Me too," Bill muttered just loud enough for everyone to hear.

"Seems to me that you might not be so impartial in this discussion, Kurt," Moose said.

"Seems to me that maybe you should let me worry about what I'm doing and let Dean worry about what he's doing."

"And if it turns out that this gives you another chance to fuck him, well then, all the better for you, right?"

"You needn't worry about Dean ending up in our bed again," Bill said, staring at his husband.

"You know what? This conversation is over," Peter said, finally stepping in to break things up. "Everyone is getting way too excited. Moose, go bowl. Kurt, go sit by your husband. Dean, I liked Tony and I'm sorry things didn't work out, but if it's over, then it's over."

Moose was about to say something else, but Peter stopped him with a wave of his hand.

"If it's over, it's over."

To no one's surprise, the boys lost all of the games that night.

* * * * *

Bill dragged Kurt home as soon as they were done bowling, begging off the drinks that the team usually had at a nearby bar. Dean, Moose and Peter left the alley and were heading to the bar when Dean stopped them.

"Look, I'm not much in the mood for going out. I think I'm

just going to head home."

"Dean, I wanted to talk to you some more about this thing with Tony," Moose said, disappointed that the evening was ending.

"Honest to God, Moose, I've got nothing left to talk about. I'm sorry if you're upset by this. I think it's absurd that you're so upset about what happened, but I am sorry."

"It's not that. It's about what you said earlier in the bowling alley. Do you really think we think less of you if you're single? You've mentioned this before and I really don't understand where it's coming from."

"I noticed a difference in how you acted towards me when I was with Tony. It was subtle, but it was there. It felt like I was one of the gang. I'm not saying you treated me badly or anything while I was single, because I wouldn't have been your friend if that was the case. I'm just saying that when I was with Tony...it was different," Dean said.

"But that's all it was, different. It wasn't better or worse, it was just different. We love you Dean, whether you're married or not. You have to know that. But I'd be lying if I didn't say that we've never seen you happier than when you were with Tony," Moose said.

Dean wanted to argue, but Moose spoke with such concern in his voice, such love, that there really wasn't anything to argue about. His friends just wanted him to be happy.

"Well, it's good to know that I'm not going to lose your friendship over this," Dean said.

"That could never happen, baby," Moose said, as he wrapped Dean in a bear hug, which lasted quite a long time. When it was over, he held Dean by the shoulders and looked at him. "We're worried about you, you know?"

"I'm worried about me too. But I'll be okay. Somehow, I always end up okay."

The emotion of the moment was getting to be too much for Dean, so he kissed his friends in quick succession and made his way off into the night.

CHAPTER 33

L
ate in the afternoon on the Saturday after bowling,
Dean was at Moose and Peter's house helping them
put up new wallpaper in the bathroom. Erik joined
them, since Terrell was in New York meeting with gallery
owners. Peter had warned Moose that he was not to get into
any arguments with Dean about Tony. Whatever else may be
going on, he told his husband, Dean was their friend and if
Moose kept hounding him about Tony he was going to drive
him away. Needless to say, Moose didn't like being told what
to do, but he agreed to at least try and be on his best behavior
when Dean was around.

"So, tell me again, why aren't we just painting this damn
room instead of putting up this nightmare wallpaper?" Erik
asked, as he balanced precariously on a ladder.

"What's wrong with the wallpaper?" Peter asked, wounded
because he had picked out the pattern.

"Nothing's wrong with it, per se, but it's a pain in the ass to
hang."

"Quit being such a princess and straighten that strip out. I swear people are going to think heterosexuals live here."

"Well, if they look at the pattern, they might," Erik muttered.

"How are things going in here?" Moose asked, popping his head in from the hallway. Peter had banned his enormous husband from the bathroom shortly after the project began.

"Great, at this pace we should be done by next Thursday," Dean said.

"This would go much quicker if you two would just do exactly what I say, when I say it," Peter said, hands on hips.

"So really, you guys have been together ten years?" Erik asked Moose.

"I think I'm just going to watch for awhile. I would kill for some popcorn right now," Moose said, as he leaned against the door. "Is that straight?"

Erik mumbled something unintelligible, yet clearly profane, as he tried once again to straighten out the wallpaper.

Dean tried not to laugh at Erik's torment. Still, it was nice to just have the urge to laugh. They had all managed to move on from Dean's announcement of the break up. Well, maybe they hadn't moved on, he thought, but at least no one was giving him grief about it. Of course, he was doing enough of that to himself.

"Done!" Erik exclaimed, a few minutes later. He stepped down of the ladder to admire his handiwork and was immediately given another strip by Peter, who waved him back up the ladder.

"So what have you guys been up to?" Moose asked Erik, as he enjoyed the suffering that his husband was putting their friends through.

"Work, work and more work. The response we've been getting to Terrell's show has been extraordinary. He's going to be huge. He's trying to keep it all in perspective though. Oh, you know what? We had dinner with Tony the other night. By the way, Dean, thanks for forgetting to tell us that you guys had split up. That provided a nice awkward moment at the beginning of the meal."

"Sorry, but there really isn't a card that you can send out to people letting them know of your break up," Dean said.

"Eh, don't worry about it. I'm sorry you guys didn't make it, you seemed like you really liked each other. Tony seemed pretty upset by the whole thing. He didn't feel much like talking about it."

"Sounds like a good plan," Dean said.

"We've become pretty good friends with him over the past few months. I asked him what happened and all he said was that you two were in different places in your life. I told him that he should keep trying with you, but he's as stubborn as you are and he said he doesn't want to push himself on you."

Erik continued to work with the wallpaper strip in his hands while he talked and therefore had no way of knowing that Dean clearly didn't want to have this conversation. Peter was staring helplessly at Moose, hoping he would do something, but Moose just watched. He wanted to see how Dean was going to respond.

"Actually, he thought you might be 'the one,'" Erik continued, oblivious to the reactions behind him. "Or the second 'the one' anyway. He's a sweet guy. Such a catch, too. Oh well, no use worrying about it. We know how you are once you've moved on from someone."

"Well, thanks for the update, but I have enough things to worry about in my life without worrying about whether or not I've ruined Tony's life too," Dean said.

"Too?" Moose asked.

"'Too' as in 'one more thing to worry about' not 'too' as in 'oh my god, what will become of me now that I've lost the great and wonderful Tony.'"

"I was just asking," Moose said, as much to Peter, who was throwing daggers at him with his eyes, as to Dean.

"Anyway, it's good to have some room to breathe again. It's nice to just be able to hang out with you guys. I feel that I've been neglecting you over the past few months. I'm sorry about that."

"Dean, we never begrudged you the time you spent with Tony. You seemed happy, so we were all happy for you, you know that," Peter said.

"Still, it's good to have my life back. I've even been neglecting Lonny, which never happened before Tony."

"Some life," Moose said, as left them to finish their work in the bathroom.

"How is Lonny?" Erik asked.

"Not good. It's really just a matter of weeks at this point. I'm amazed I can say it without bursting into tears, but the last few weeks have made me realize that it's coming. You can hear it in his voice. I could see it in his face when we were down there. He sounds so tired. You know Lonny, he's always so upbeat, so energetic. To hear him like this really hurts."

"Are you planning on seeing him before...anytime soon?" Erik asked.

"Yeah, I'm going down there next weekend. His mom seems to have forgiven me for driving her crazy. I honestly don't know what I'm going to do when he's gone. I have this sense of acceptance about it right now, but I don't think it's going to last. I can't imagine a world where I don't get to talk to him every day. I mean, he's been a part of my life for almost thirty years. It's like I'm losing part of myself. When Tony and I were down there, I was trying to explain to him how alone I'm going to be when Lonny dies, and he just didn't get it."

"Well, maybe that's because Tony didn't think you would be so alone. He thought you would still be together," Moose said. He had reappeared at the door and had been listening to them talk.

"Strip," Erik said to Dean, who looked at him with utter confusion. "Wallpaper, honey. I need another strip. I think I'm finally getting the hang of this."

"Dean, when Lonny finally does...go...maybe you should stay with us for awhile. Take some time off work. You can stay in the guest bedroom. I don't think it will be such a good idea for you to be alone," Peter said.

"Thanks, sweetie, but I can't. I've been taking too many days off, here and there, to visit Lonny and do other things. Plus, I'll need to go down for the funeral. It's all so surreal."

"Moose, do you remember when Jerry Merkland died?" Erik asked.

"God, there's a blast from the past. That was, like, 15 years ago?" Moose asked, a bit of wonder in his voice realizing that so many years had passed.

"I was such a wreck when that happened. I don't think we knew you yet, Peter. Jerry was one of the regular crew. It was so unreal. You know, once we all made it through the eighties and were into the nineties, I thought we were home free. Then Jerry goes to work one morning and has an aneurism. I don't think I left my house for anything other than work for almost six months."

"That was the worst part, the suddenness of it all," Moose said. "I think I had grown so accustomed to people dying slowly that I had forgotten that sometimes people could just be yanked away from you."

"Well, trust me, sometimes a slow death isn't so great either," Dean said.

"No, there was so much left unsaid, so much that I wish I would have told him before he died," Erik said. "It may not seem like it know, Dean, but believe me, someday you'll be grateful that you had the chance to say goodbye."

CHAPTER 34

I n the end, no one got the chance to say goodbye to Lonny. Not really. The following afternoon, while Dean and Erik and everyone else were enjoying the barbeque at Moose and Peter's house, Lonny died. He had woken up that morning feeling feverish, but nothing so bad that they felt the need to take him to the hospital. After lunch, he played *Chutes and Ladders* with his nieces while his father watched basketball and his sister and mother made Sunday dinner. Around two in the afternoon, he went to take a nap. And that was that. When Donny went to wake him, he was already gone.

It was early evening in Florida by the time everything had been situated and the family began making calls. Dean was sitting at Moose and Peter's picnic table having a conversation with Bill and Erik when his phone rang. He saw that it was Lonny's parents' number on the caller ID and his blood went cold. He knew. He *knew*.

One by one, his friends fell silent around him as Dean spoke to Donny. The conversation was quiet, and Dean said very little. He hung up the phone and stared at it.

"Dean?" Moose asked, knowing already what the news was going to be.

Dean looked up at Moose and burst into tears. Soon, everyone who knew Lonny was crying and hugging each other. They had all been through this too many times before. Even though everyone was dealing with their own pain, most of their support and attention was focused on Dean, because they knew that he had lost the most.

The crying eventually turned to telling stories about Lonny which eventually turned to laughter. Tears came and went over the course of the night, but everyone could see that Dean was having an incredibly difficult time. Peter again asked him to stay at their house, but again, he refused. By the time Erik dropped him off at his apartment, he was drained. He lay down and expected to fall asleep, but instead, the tears came again and kept going until morning.

* * * * *

By Tuesday afternoon, when he, Moose and Peter arrived in Jacksonville, Dean had managed a grand total of four hours sleep. For all of his preparation, for all of his talk about acceptance, he actually felt like he was going crazy. Well, crazier, really. When he tried to sleep, his mind went into overdrive with thoughts of Lonny, his parents, the friends he'd lost over the years, and Tony.

It was interesting that amid all the thoughts of death and loss, he kept circling back to Tony. The one brief sleep that he was able to get, he even dreamed of Tony. They were together in London and the dream brought on a feeling of such heartbreaking happiness that Dean actually gasped when he woke up. Then the tears started falling again.

The funeral was a thing of beauty. Lonny had made it very clear to his family that he didn't want a sad funeral. There were pictures of Lonny scattered throughout the church. Hundreds of pictures from every stage of his life. Donny eulogized him in the way that only a father can truly remember his son. There were tears, but for the most part, they were tears of joy from a life remembered. Dean managed to pull himself together long enough to speak about their friendship. His voice cracked once, and he almost lost it, but he made it through. When he was finished, he sat back down between Moose and Peter, his friends using their bodies as shields to try and ward off the pain that he was going through.

Everyone gathered at Donny and Connie's house after the funeral. It was, as these things go, a great party. In keeping with Lonny's wishes, everyone was determined to remember the joyousness of his life. When one family member or friend would start to fall apart, others would gather around and tell a story about Lonny that would inevitably bring a laugh or a smile. There was only so much cheering up Dean could take, however, and he finally had to get out.

"Where are you going?" Moose asked.

"I'm just going outside for a bit. I'm tired and I'm on sensory overload. I just need some space."

"I'll come with you."

"Moose, I'll be fine. I'm just going to get some air for a few minutes."

Dean made his way out the sliding glass doors at the back of the house. The Turnow house had a beautiful deck and swimming pool, as well as an enormous garden in the back yard. He went around to the side of the house where Connie and Donny had built a small oasis of calm. A wicker loveseat was nestled next to a fountain and hidden away from the rest of the yard by large rubber tree plants. The late afternoon sky had turned dark and gray, which had cooled things down. It was a welcome relief from the heat that had already taken hold, even though it was only mid-spring.

Earlier, as everyone was leaving the funeral, Donny had encouraged them to take whatever pictures they wanted, whatever pictures would bring them joy when they remembered Lonny. Dean reached into his jacket pocket and pulled out the picture that he had taken. The picture was of him and Lonny when they were thirteen years old. Dean had joined the Turnows on a weekend trip to a lake house one summer. In the picture, he and Lonny were shirtless, wearing cut off shorts, their hair wet and tousled after a dip in the lake. They were mugging for the camera and their faces were filled with such unfettered happiness, that Dean couldn't help but smile.

"A picture really is worth a thousand words," Connie said, briefly startling Dean. She sat down on the loveseat next to him and looked at the snapshot he was holding. "Oh, I love that one. You two were just inseparable. It feels like you've been a part of this family forever."

Dean sat quietly, not trusting himself to say anything.

"Here's another one you might like," Connie said, as she handed a picture to Dean. It took him a moment to realize that it was of him and Lonny the night before Christmas Eve, laughing on the couch in the family room.

"How did you get this?" Dean asked in amazement.

"You boys were never as quiet as you thought you were," she said, mischievously. "I heard you two in there that night and I got up to join you. When I saw you giggling like two schoolgirls, I knew I just had to get a picture. Once I did, I just went back to bed. It was wonderful seeing Lonny so happy and I didn't want to break the spell."

Dean stared at the pictures in his hands. The bookends of his life with Lonny. Again, he was overwhelmed by the sense of loss he was feeling. He couldn't help but wonder how, after losing so many people over so many years, he could still feel so devastated. Surely, he had to reach a point were he would just be numb to all of the pain.

"I came out here for another reason," Connie said, interrupting Dean's thoughts. "Lonny actually had a last request. Listening to people talk today, I guess I was never aware that my son had such a flair for the theatrical."

Dean laughed softly, "Yeah, Lonny liked a good show."

"After he died, I found a note and two letters. One to you

and one to your friend Tony. Lonny asked me to mail them before you came down for the funeral. They should be there when you get back to Chicago."

Dean laughed again and shook his head. Only Lonny. His pain notwithstanding, he wished Lonny were here just so that he could throttle him.

"What's so funny?" Connie asked.

"Nothing. It's typical Lonny. Far be it for him to let a little thing like death keep him from meddling in my love life."

"What's to meddle? You two seemed very happy when you were here a few weeks ago. Is everything okay?"

"Nothing worth worrying over," Dean said. Lonny hadn't told his mother that he and Tony were no longer together, he realized.

"Well, I'm glad for that." Connie said. "He is such a charming man, and you light up when you're around him. Don't take anything for granted, Dean. You never know when it is going to be taken away from you."

Knowing she was on the verge of tears, Connie stood up to leave. "Don't stay out here too much longer, honey. There is a whole house full of people in there who love you and you should be in there with them."

"I'll be in soon," Dean promised.

He sat quietly for a few minutes after she left, staring at the pictures. Connie was right, he should go inside. He should be with his friends. He should allow them to help him get through this horrible time. He should be like everyone else and grieve and laugh and find a way to move on.

But he wasn't like everyone else. Tonight, Connie would lie down next to Donny and he would hold her until the sun came up. Moose and Peter would do the same thing. Back in Chicago, Erik and Terrell and Kurt and Bill would do the same. Even someone like Tony, who had to live through the loss of a husband, had his family to lean on. Dean was alone. Mind numbingly, heart achingly, seemingly never endingly alone. No one got it. No one understood what it was like to feel so isolated. He knew it was partly his own fault. He could probably show up on Tony's doorstep when he returned to Chicago and start over. But that wasn't in his nature. His reasons for breaking up with Tony had been a jumbled mess, but it was done, and for Dean there was no going back.

CHAPTER 35

Terrell and Erik were waiting at O'Hare just outside the
security checkpoint when the boys returned home on
Thursday afternoon. There was a long group hug when
they arrived.

"You look like shit, baby," Terrell said to Dean. They all
looked exhausted, but Dean looked like he had been put
through the wringer.

"You cry for five days and come see me," Dean said, as
hoisted his bag up on to his shoulder. "Let's get out of here. I
feel like I could sleep for a solid week."

They made their way through the underground
passageways to the parking garage. The five of them squeezed
into Terrell's Lexus and began the long drive into the city.

"Lonny's mother asked me to thank you guys for the
flowers," Dean said to Terrell. "They were really beautiful."

"I wish we could have been there. It's probably for the best
though. I doubt his family wanted a gaggle of homo's
descending on them from Chicago."

"How was New York?" Moose asked.

"Great. I've got a show lined up at one of the galleries in July. It's pretty amazing. It's been such a whirlwind. I just got back yesterday. Erik and I had dinner with Tony last night," Terrell said, directing his last comment to Dean who was avoiding eye contact in the back seat. "He sends his regards. He felt terrible when we told him about Lonny."

"Well, tell him to be on the lookout for a letter from the great beyond," Dean said. There was an edge in his voice that worried Moose.

"Are you okay?" Moose asked.

"I'm fine. I'm just exhausted. And frankly, the last thing I feel like doing is talking about Tony."

"Sorry," Terrell said. "I was just making conversation. What do you mean by 'the great beyond'?"

Dean hadn't told Moose or Peter about the letters Lonny had sent, so he filled everyone in on the conversation that he'd had with Connie.

"Leave it to Lonny," Peter said, with a chuckle.

"Yeah, he must have loved Tony just as much as the rest of you. Maybe you can all go have dinner with him after you drop me off at the apartment."

"Seriously, what's the matter with you?" Moose asked again.

"Like I said, I'm exhausted. Also, if you listened to that story carefully, you'd realize that I've got a letter waiting for me too, which I'm not all that thrilled about reading. I don't need advice from one more person about how to handle my life. Especially someone I can't argue with."

"No, I don't think that's it. You've been acting weird since yesterday. You seem very withdrawn. Even for you," Moose said.

"Well, that's my modus operandi, isn't it? I'm done crying. I'm done being upset. I'm done. I just want to move on."

When they reached Dean's apartment, Moose got out to let Dean out of the car.

"Give me a few minutes," Moose said to Terrell.

"I don't need help with the bag, Moose. Go home. You've got to be just as tired as I am," Dean said. He wanted desperately to be alone.

Moose ignored him and grabbed his bag and began walking to the door. Dean just sighed and followed him. Once inside the entranceway, he got his mail, and let Moose in through the second door that led to the stairs to his apartment.

"So, is the letter there?" Moose asked when they were inside.

"Yes, but I'm not going to open it right now."

"Do you remember our Christmas party? When Lonny came up?" Moose suddenly asked.

"Yes. What about it?"

"At one point in the evening, you saw me and Lonny talking and you came over and asked us what was going on."

"Yes, and you both lied and said you weren't talking about anything important. Again, what about it?"

"You know, Dean, your tone is getting old. Anyway, we were talking about you. Even though he told you he wasn't going to tell anyone, Lonny told me that night that he was dying. He was very worried about you and what would happen once he died. Not that he needed to tell me, but he mentioned that you aren't as strong as you seem."

"Well, I'll give him that one," Dean said.

"So he asked me to look out for you – again, not something he needed to do."

"Moose, I'm fine. I've been through hell. I've just lost my best friend in the world. I don't know what you want from me. I will get through this and life will go on. If you're worried that I'm going to do something stupid, you can relax."

"I'm not worried about that at all. It's just that we all love you. And we're all worried about you. As hard as this is for us, we know that it has to be a hundred times harder for you. I want you to know that we're here for you. Talk to us. Cry on our shoulders. Yell at us. Do something. But don't do the withdrawal thing that you're doing now. It's not healthy and it's not fair – to you or to us."

"Honey, I love you and I appreciate everything you're saying and everything that you're trying to do, but I've got nothing left. Maybe someday, but not now. I'm numb down to my core. I know myself pretty well and I know that it's going to take every ounce of strength that I have just to get through the next few weeks."

"Okay. I just wanted to put it out there," Moose said. He could tell that any further discussion would be pointless. "There's one more thing. Peter and I are thinking of having everyone over for dinner some time next week, just to get some normalcy back into all of our lives."

"Sounds great. I'll see what work is like and then I'll let you know," Dean said, refusing to commit to anything.

"And by everyone, I also mean Tony," Moose said carefully.

"That's fine," Dean said, smiling at the look on Moose's face. "You thought I would say that I wasn't going to be there if you invited Tony?"

"Well, I didn't know how you would react, honestly."

"I know you all like Tony, and I'm sure he'll be around us from time to time. No sense in making a drama of it. Lord knows enough of our friends are people that I dated or slept with at one time or another."

"Great. And who knows, maybe you guys can start over again."

"If I had any strength at all, I would clock you upside the head. Do you really think that I'm in any condition to date someone?"

"No, not right now, but who knows what the future holds. He's a really great guy, you know – he's not just 'someone.'"

"Yes, yes, yes," Dean said, finally having had enough, "Tony is great and fabulous and the best thing that ever happened to me. I'm nothing without him – well at least according you and everyone else I know."

"Again with this? You're one of the nicest, sweetest guys

that any of us has ever met. You're kind and caring and so decent sometimes it hurts. You're all of that and more. But when you were with Tony, you were also happy."

Dean just stared. "You should go now."

"Look, I'll call you later tonight," Moose said, and then he was gone.

Dean shook his head and sat down on the couch and started flipping through the mail, until finally he came across Lonny's letter. In typical Lonny fashion, the penmanship on the front of the letter was impeccable, while on the back were various *Dora the Explorer* stickers he pilfered from his nieces. Dean couldn't help but laugh, which was no doubt Lonny's goal. He flipped the letter over in his hands a few times before finally getting up the courage to open it.

> *Dear DeeDee –*
>
> *If you are reading this letter, I must be dead. Oh, C'mon! Who wouldn't want to start a letter that way?*
>
> *Sorry, had a little giggle fit there for a second. I don't know if I ever mentioned it, but the drugs they give me for the pain are fabulous!*
>
> *Before you read any further, I feel that I should warn you about something – I AM IN THE ROOM WITH YOU RIGHT NOW! Oh, yeah, that's right! I'm watching you – and if you so much as think about rolling your eyes, I will go poltergeist on your ass. Don't try me.*
>
> *If Mother followed my instructions correctly, you're home from the funeral, sitting on that couch of yours that I've always hated (I can say these things now – what are you going to do?) wondering what the fuck you're going to do now that I'm gone.*
>
> *Believe it or not, you're going to be fine. For all of your sense of gloom and doom about the world and the shit that life has continually thrown at you, you never really understood how good you have it. You*

have probably the greatest group of friends in the world, and they love you more than you can imagine (in spite of yourself). Don't push them away, Dean. Pull them closer. They are the only ones that will get you through this.

There's one other thing you need to do. As the immortal philosopher Madonna once said, "Open Your Heart." I could kick your ass for dumping Tony. He loves you. You love him. It is the simplest thing in the world, and you insist on making it so complicated. As Mother no doubt told you, I also sent a letter to Tony. Want to know what I told him? Go over there and ask him! HA! He's the one, DeeDee. Look in your heart and you'll know it as well as everyone else does.

It's getting late here, and I'm a bit tired. I want you to know that you were the greatest thing that ever happened to me. My life may have been short, but because of you, it was definitely sweet. I wish you all the love and happiness in the world, Dean, because no one deserves it more than you. And the great thing is that everything you have ever wanted is right there waiting for you – all you have to do is find the strength to grab it.

Take care of yourself, Dean. You always were and always will be, my best friend.

Love,
Lonny

Dean set the letter down on the coffee table and stared at the ceiling. He wanted to cry, but he had nothing left. He wanted to scream at the top of his lungs about the unfairness of it all, but there was no voice within him. More than anything, he wanted to believe Lonny. He wanted to believe that he could love someone and be loved by him in return. He wanted to believe that all the happiness he had ever hoped for was just around the corner, waiting for him to reach out and take it. But he knew better. He was broken in some way that he couldn't fully explain to anyone. It wasn't that he didn't deserve happiness – he just wasn't wired for it.

CHAPTER 36

Dean woke up Friday morning after the first full night's sleep he had had in over a week only to find that he was in worse shape than ever. The exhaustion had apparently been a blessing in disguise because now that he was more rested, he felt like he was crawling out of his skin. From the moment he opened his eyes, all he could do was think about Lonny. It occurred to him that at any other time, he would call Lonny and talk to him about what was bothering him. The realization that that would never happen again was almost too much for him to bear.

His friends called, one by one, and he lied to all of them. He said he was fine and that he was just resting. Pride or stupidity prevented him from opening up and letting anyone know that he was in bad shape. By late afternoon, he was just about to lose it completely when salvation came from a most unexpected place.

"Hey, babe, how are you doing?" Kurt asked.

"I'm fine," Dean lied. "Actually, I'm a bit stir-crazy, but other than that I'm doing fine."

"Fine, huh?"

"As well as can be expected, I suppose."

"Listen, Bill and I aren't doing anything. Why don't you come over? We can have dinner, watch a movie. Just hang out. We'd love to see you."

"You know what? That sounds great. I really do need to get out of here. Let me hop in the shower and I'll be over in a little while. Thanks, by the way."

"Don't worry about it. We'll see you soon, handsome."

He knew that seeing Kurt was probably not the solution to what was going on inside his head. But he also knew that he didn't care. It was a stupid decision that was made easier by the three vodka-cranberries he had already downed. Ultimately, the thought of someone holding him right now was just too much for his booze soaked brain to resist.

* * * * *

"Hola, amigos," Dean said. He tripped slightly as he entered their house, giggling as he did. "I brought wine, but I may not really need anything more to drink."

Bill smiled at Dean, who was hanging on Kurt. "Let me take that. How are you feeling?"

"A little drunk."

"Besides that, I mean," Bill said.

"Honestly, I'm so tired of talking about everything," Dean said. "Can we just not talk about it all? No Lonny. No Tony. No more talk of anything heavy. I just need to escape for a while."

The things that Dean didn't want to talk about made for perhaps the largest pink elephant in the room ever. Still, the threesome managed to make it through the late afternoon and into the evening with no drama. They even managed to muster up a few laughs. The dinner was great, even though Bill and Kurt both worried about Dean's continued alcohol consumption. Through his haze, Dean was surprised how well they were all getting along. He was worried how Bill might react to his presence, but he seemed to be fine – which was a good thing, considering what he was really up to.

"I'm going to go make some coffee," Bill said.

"Sounds great. C'mon babe, let's go find a movie to watch," Kurt said.

Dean was slightly unsteady on his feet as he followed Kurt into the living room. He watched as Kurt went over to the entertainment center to find a movie. It wasn't perfect, and it probably wasn't the smartest idea, but it would do. For one night, he didn't want to think about anything. He just wanted to be with someone.

"Maybe we should just forget about the movie and go to bed," Dean said, closing the distance between them.

"Now, now, be good," Kurt said. He sounded nervous, which took Dean by surprise. But he assumed it was because was worried about how Bill would react.

"Don't play hard to get. Think of it as helping out a friend. I'm sure Bill won't mind. We'll even let him join us," Dean said with a giggle, as he tried to unbutton Kurt's shirt.

"Dean, please stop," Kurt said. He grabbed both of Dean's hands and held him away. "We don't do that anymore."

"Who are *we* and what aren't *we* doing anymore?" Dean asked.

"*We* are me and Kurt," Bill said from the doorway. Dean was momentarily embarrassed by having been caught with his hands almost in the cookie jar, but the look of pity on Bill's face quickly began turning his embarrassment to anger.

"Do you remember that night that Bill walked out on me at Charlie's? Well, he almost walked out on me for good. We were up until dawn talking. It was everything I could do to convince him to stay, not that I would have blamed him if he'd left," Kurt said, with an affectionate look toward his husband that made Dean's blood run cold. "Bill and I need to focus on our relationship for awhile. Despite my jackass-like behavior, he means everything to me. I don't know what I would have done if I'd lost him – and I don't ever want to feel that feeling again."

"Oh really? You seemed to jump to my defense that night at bowling when I told everyone that Tony and I had broken up," Dean said.

"True, but that wasn't about sleeping with you. I think I was just angry at Moose. He can be a bit holier-than-thou sometimes and it was pissing me off," Kurt said.

"Dean, I know that you're going through a lot right now, and this probably isn't what you were expecting when you came over tonight, but we hope you understand what we're saying here," Bill said, as he came over and stood next to Kurt.

"Are you fucking kidding me with this?" Dean asked. He was on fire now and there was no way to stop it. "Do you guys have some magic monogamy on-off switch that you flick when it's convenient? This is such bullshit."

"There's something else," Kurt said, hoping to calm things down. "As hard as it is to keep a relationship going, I guess I'd forgotten how hard it is to get one off the ground. I'm really sorry for how I was acting when you were with Tony. I know I didn't make things easy for you two, and I wish you knew how terrible I feel about it now. For what's it worth, with hindsight and all, Tony seems like a great guy. Who knows? Maybe you two..."

"Oh please!" Dean screamed, "You're giving me relationship advice? Seriously? You guys are un-fucking-real. You take what you need and then when someone needs something from you, you just leave him hanging. You guys can go fuck yourselves. Oh wait! That's your new plan. I'm out of here."

"Dean, wait. Please don't go. Not like this," Bill said. The last thing he wanted was Dean running around in the streets in his condition. "Let's just sit down and have some coffee. We've been friends for a long time. We don't want you to leave like this."

"I'm pretty good at losing people," Dean said as he reached

the door. "Believe me, I'll survive."

* * * * *

Dean stormed and staggered his way to the first bar he could find. A few drinks later, he was angrier than ever. His cell phone rang at least half a dozen times and he ignored it. The bartender finally cut him off and called him a cab. He really did think he was going crazy and he wasn't sure if he even cared anymore. Still, he couldn't bear to go home to his empty apartment. He gave the cab driver Moose and Peter's address and tried not to throw up on the drive there.

Ten minutes later, Dean stumbled up the front steps of the house in which he had spent so many wonderful moments in his life. But even this place of unconditional love wasn't bringing him any comfort tonight. He rang the doorbell and steadied himself against the wall for support.

"Jesus Christ, Dean, where have you been?" Moose asked after opening the door. "We've been calling you for an hour."

"That was you? I thought it was that asshole, Kurt," Dean said as he tripped into the foyer. He turned around and steadied himself against the wall and saw that Moose had been joined by Peter.

"You guys are not going to believe this! So I go over to Kurt and Bill's house for dinner..."

"We know, Dean, they called us as soon as you left," Bill said, interrupting Dean. "That's why we've been trying to reach you. We've been worried sick. Are you okay?"

"Oh, I'm just great. I can count the people who care about me in this world on one hand, but otherwise, I'm doing fucking fantastic."

"Honey, you need to calm down. We're trying to tell you something."

But Dean wasn't listening. "Oh man, you guys must love this! Well, I'm officially completely and totally alone. Everyone better lock up their husbands. Did you guys know about this little monogamy pact of theirs? A fucking heads up would have been nice!"

Dean moved into the living room with Moose and Peter hot on his tail. He was just about to turn back towards them and continue his tirade when he was stopped dead in his tracks by the sight of Tony standing next to the fireplace.

"Oh my god, this day gets better and better!" Dean yelled.

"Calm down, Dean. Tony was already here," Kurt said.

"I'm sure he was. Did I interrupt anything? Were you guys about to hit the sack? He's great in bed you know. You won't regret it."

"Careful Dean," Tony warned.

"You need to leave now," Dean said coldly.

"No one's going anywhere," Moose said.

"He goes, or I go," Dean said, on the verge of tears.

"Dean, calm down," Bill said, as he moved towards him.

"Just stop," Dean said, backing away and tumbling onto the couch, the tears flowing freely now. "I can't lose you guys too. I've lost too much. Lonny's gone. Tony's gone. I can't lose everything."

Tony's anger had already turned to concern when he realized the state Dean was in. But it was an entirely different feeling – one that he didn't even know how to characterize – that he felt upon hearing the regret in Dean's voice over their breakup. He looked at Moose and Bill, and they seemed as surprised as he was.

Questions would have to wait, however, because Dean's crying had stopped as quickly as it had started. Passing out will do that.

CHAPTER 37

In the beginning, there was the light – and it was not good. Dean groaned as he woke up and pulled the comforter up over his eyes. While the cover provided some relief from the light, the actual movement involved in pulling it over his head caused the headache he was currently experiencing to blaze like a supernova between his temples. He waited for the pain to pass and then slowly lowered the cover and looked around the room. He had no idea where he was. The room looked vaguely familiar, but he couldn't quite place it. And good God, the place reeked. A moment or two later, he realized that the stench in the room was emanating from himself.

He swung his legs over the side of the bed and held on for dear life as the world went spinning. Oh, this is not good, he thought. His stomach did flip-flops, and for just a moment, he thought he was going to throw up. Judging by the raw feeling in his throat, he guessed that he had already done as much of that as he was going to do.

Standing up slowly, Dean leaned against the bed and tried to focus. A noise of to his left caught his attention and he turned to see a tree branch scraping against a small window. Then it hit him. He was at Tony's house in Saugatuck. Unexpectedly, a brief shot of joy coursed through him. It faded just as fast when he realized that he was in one of the guest bedrooms, not Tony's room.

He slowly made his way down the hallway towards the living room, holding on to the walls for support.

"Hello?" Dean said.

"It lives," Tony said, from behind. Dean turned and was momentarily blinded by the light, as Tony was standing in the sliding glass doors that led out to the lake.

"Barely," Dean mumbled, turning back towards the kitchen to protect his eyes. "Is there coffee?"

"There was eight hours ago when I got up, it's a little past three in the afternoon now, however."

"Oy. Where is everyone?"

"There is no everyone. It's just the two of us."

Dean cocked his eyebrow and gave a little smile at that bit of news.

"You can relax, you're perfectly safe. That's why I put you in the guest bedroom," Tony said. There wasn't any judgment or disdain in what he'd said, but for some reason, Dean couldn't help but feel disappointed.

"Mind if I make some coffee?" Dean asked.

"How about I make some coffee and you go take a shower. I'm begging you," Tony said, with a laugh.

"I might need a Silkwood scrub down to get all of this out of me," Dean said, taking another whiff of himself.

"How much of yesterday do you remember?" Tony asked, delicately.

"Hmm?"

"You were pretty drunk when I brought you up here. Unconscious, actually. How much do you remember?"

Dean tried to focus on what might have happened yesterday. It was all a blur. He remembered going over to Kurt and Bill's house. That first memory was all it took and the rest of the day came rushing back to him in a flood of humiliation.

"Jesus Christ," Dean said, his face turning red.

"So, I gather, you remember most of it," Tony said, again without judgment.

Dean couldn't face him. "How did I end up here?"

"You went a little crazy at Moose and Peter's house. Then you passed out. We talked about what to do with you, and I convinced them to let me bring you here, that way you couldn't escape."

"What, *Hazelden* was too far a drive?"

"Well, I don't think you're quite that far gone. However, I have hidden all the booze, so if you start getting jittery, let me know."

"I can't imagine wanting anything less in the world right now than a drink of alcohol."

"That's a good sign, I suppose," Tony said.

"Listen, let me shower up and you can take me back to the city. After everything that's happened, I'm sure the last thing you want to do is baby-sit me."

"I know how much you love to make decisions, but I think I'm going to take that one out of your hands. You're staying the night. I need to feel that I'm doing something to help you."

"Why? I mean after everything I've done, why do you even care? I'd think you'd be getting a kick out of this."

"And I think you know me better than that."

"True. So why?" Dean asked.

"Because I want to get to the bottom of this. We may not have any sort of future together, but I still love you, Dean. And as someone who loves you, I can't just stand by and watch what's happening to you. You're falling apart and its breaking my heart."

Dean was once again at a loss for words. "I'm going to go take a shower."

Several minutes later, the hot water was blasting down on him, slowly leeching the alcohol from his body. The water would have had to have been laced with Demerol to make him forget everything that happened yesterday, however. He would have thought that being so drunk he would have some trouble remembering what an ass he'd made of himself, but it was all stored safely in his brain, playing itself out over and over. How could he have lost it like that? I'm sure the boys in Chicago are burning up the phone lines about this one, he thought.

The door to the bathroom opened and Tony walked in. For just a moment Dean's heart fluttered because he absurdly thought Tony was going to join him.

"I washed your clothes from yesterday," Tony said, yelling over the water.

"Thanks," Dean said. "For everything."

"Don't worry about it," Tony said, closing the door behind him.

Even after everything that had happened, Dean was amazed by the effect that Tony still had on him. To be naked and so close to him, with only a flimsy shower curtain separating them was almost too much for him to take. He couldn't help but wonder what would have happened if he would have invited Tony in to wash his back. Probably nothing. Tony was a lot of things, but as his friends had pointed out, he was just as stubborn as Dean was.

He realized that more than anything he wished he could talk to Lonny about all of this. That caused the tears to start falling again, but not for quite as long this time.

* * * * *

"You look almost human again," Tony said, when Dean emerged from the bathroom twenty minutes later. "Did you get soap in your eyes?"

"Yeah," Dean lied.

"Moose called. He wanted to make sure that you were okay. I think he wanted to come up, but I convinced him that you'd be fine for one night up here alone."

Tony handed Dean a cup of coffee, made just the way he

liked it, which he accepted gratefully. Tony then went over to start a fire. Dean was surprised by the unseasonably cold weather. This being the Midwest, that probably meant it would be ninety degrees and humid by tomorrow afternoon. He couldn't help but think they looked like a gay coffee ad with Tony tending the fire while he sipped his coffee. These are indeed the moments of our lives. Dean laughed out loud and almost spilled his coffee.

"What's so funny?" Tony asked, smiling at Dean and grateful for the change in his mood.

"Nothing, just having a bit of a surreal moment," Dean said as he made his way over to the couch.

"Well, it's nice to see you laughing again, but don't even think about sitting down," Tony said.

"Why? Is that some sort of bizarre AA ritual? No sitting until you're sober for twenty-four hours?"

"Stop it, Dean, you're not an alcoholic," Tony said, with a laugh. "You are, however, a great cook and you are going to march into the kitchen and start making dinner. I'm starving."

"See how you are? I'm sad and vulnerable and you're making me your kitchen bitch."

Tony laughed and continued playing with the fire. Dean stopped and looked at him. He was struck once again by how much things had changed between them – and how much they hadn't.

"Tony, why are you doing this?"

"I thought we covered that."

"What I mean is, what are you hoping to get out of this? What do you want from me?"

"Believe it or not, Dean, I really don't have any ulterior motives. Who knows what will ultimately become of you and me? Honestly, that isn't my concern right now. When Steve died, there were so many people there for me. I guess I just want to return the favor for someone else. For one night, I want you to let go and let someone else carry whatever burden it is you think you're carrying. I want you to just relax and know that you can say anything and I'm not going to question you or judge you. I think you need someone to talk to, and I want that person to be me."

More than anything in the world, Dean wanted to walk over to Tony and bury his head in his chest and hold him forever. Instead, he smiled a sad smile and continued on to the kitchen. He just didn't have it in himself to tell Tony everything he was feeling. To open himself up so completely to anyone was almost impossible. But Tony? Deep down he knew that despite all the concern he was showing and all the nice things he was saying, he had done too much for Tony to ever really care about him again.

CHAPTER 38

"**H**ave you ever thought about opening a restaurant?" Tony asked. He finally had to force himself to push his plate out of arm's reach. "I only bought staples when I was in town, how on earth did you turn that into a four-star meal?"

"You're sweet, but I would hardly call that four-star," Dean said, as he began clearing the table.

"Still the master of gracefully accepting compliments, I see," Tony chided.

"Some things never change," Dean said.

"Some things do. You seem more relaxed. I haven't seen you like this since, well, the last time you were up here."

"Maybe instead of being a chef, I should be a Saugatuck houseboy. You head back to the city and I'll just hang out here. I promise everything will be squeaky clean whenever you come for a weekend"

"I'm not that rich," Tony replied

Dean had to admit that he was feeling pretty good. He and Tony had talked and laughed and carried on through dinner as if there had never been any bad blood between them. Still, he had to remind himself that this wasn't reality. Eventually he would have to go back to the city and deal with work and his friends and all of the wreckage of his life.

"Uh oh, you've got the frowny face," Tony said.

"Yeah. Just giving myself an internal reality check. Thirty-six hours from now, it's back to work. Back to everything. You know, Lonny used to call me every morning. I can't imagine sitting at my desk and not hearing that phone ring. I just don't know what my life is going to be like now. Especially after I've humiliated myself in front of almost everyone I know."

"You don't really think your friends care about what happened yesterday? The only thing I felt from them was concern about you."

"Oh, I'm sure there'll be years of 'Hey, remember when Dean had his nervous breakdown' stories."

"You care way too much about what people think about you, Dean. Everyone is allowed to lose control sometimes."

"Have you met me?" Dean asked with a laugh. He poured a couple of cups of coffee and handed one to Tony. "I'm going to go sit by the fireplace. My body is still a bit out of whack."

"I can't believe how cold it is," Tony said, as he followed Dean into the living room. "It feels like its going to rain, too. Great sleeping weather."

As they settled in by the fireplace, Dean collected his thoughts. So much about himself had been exposed in the last few days, he decided, that he might as well go all the way.

"I owe you an apology," Dean said, quietly.

"For what?"

"You were right about me breaking up with you. I think I was looking for a reason to end things that night I came over. I should have been more honest with you. I should have just taken a step back. I should have done a lot of things. Instead, I was a dick. You're a great guy, Tony, and you deserved better."

"Better than you? Or better than the way you treated me

that night?"

"Both, I suppose."

"Nah. I'll give you one of those, but not the other. You were the best thing that happened to me in a long time, Dean, and I don't regret a minute of what we had."

Dean was surprised by how much Tony's use of the past tense hurt him. Oh well, you reap what you sow, he thought. Not to mention the fact that he was still so mentally fucked up that the last thing he should do was try to get back together with Tony. He really did deserve better, whether he realized it or not.

"So why haven't you asked about Lonny's letter?" Tony asked.

"Oh, I'm pretty sure I know what it said. He's difficult, but he has a good heart. Give him time. Don't give up. Blah blah blah."

"Not quite," Tony said, as he got up and walked into the kitchen where one of his bags was sitting. He pulled out Lonny's letter and brought it over to Dean. "I don't think he'd mind if I let you read it."

Dean set his coffee down and once again found himself flipping over and over in his hands a letter from his best friend. Tony casually rested his arm behind Dean, as if to protect him from whatever emotions he might experience from what Lonny had written. Dean took a deep breath and opened the letter.

Dear Tony –

Well, this is quite a pickle you've gotten yourself into, isn't it? Falling in love with our little DeeDee? He's a handful, isn't he? Grouchy one minute; sunshine and roses the next. What were you thinking?

Seriously, though, you must be a very special man, because I think you've been able to see what everyone sees, but doesn't fully appreciate – Dean is an extraordinary human being. The truth is, he's the greatest guy I've ever known and he doesn't even have a clue as to how wonderful he really is.

I'm not just talking about the financial support he's given me over the years – which no one knows about, by the way – but the fact that he never judged me for being who I am, for living the kind of wild, outside the lines life that I lived. He just loved me and supported me, like he does everyone.

I'll be honest, when Dean first told me that you two had started dating, I didn't have very high hopes. After all, I've known him for a lot of years and I've seen him burn through a lot of guys. But the more he talked about you, the more I realized that you were the one. Then, when you two came down here, I knew it. I could see it in the way you looked at each other, the way you acted around each other. It was beautiful.

True to form, of course, Dean fucked it up. I'd like to say that I'm surprised, but one should never tell a lie this close to dying – bad karma, you know.

Ultimately, the problem was that you simply got too close to his heart. Dean has been alone for so long that I think that it's the only thing he knows how to do. He's lost so many people in his life that I think that is the only way he thinks relationships can end. He has the biggest heart I've ever seen, despite everything he's been through, but he keeps himself closed off, thinking it will somehow protect him. All it really does is isolate him more. You'd think he'd be smart enough to realize this – especially considering how many times I've told him over the years – but you'd be wrong.

So why am I telling you all of this? The truth is I think you need him as much as he needs you. I know I don't know you all that well, but I wish you could see the way you look at Dean. It's amazing. After I'm gone, I'm pretty sure Dean is going to fall apart. I was his touchstone and he's going to have a hard time without me.

Whatever happens, please be there for Dean, even if it is only as a friend. He can be a lot of work, but as I think you already know, he's worth it. I wish I could have gotten to know you better, Tony, because you seem like a great guy. I wish you all the happiness in the world.

Love,
Lonny

Dean took his time refolding the letter, trying hard to maintain his composure. The last thing he wanted was to have yet another crying jag. This was the last that he would ever hear from Lonny and it broke his heart all over again.

"I'm sorry about that," Dean said.

"About what?" Tony asked, confused.

"He had no right to ask you to look after me. Especially after everything that happened. He was always a pesky meddler, bless his heart," Dean said, as he tried to blink away the tears that refused to obey him.

"I think you missed the point of the letter. Or at least the point that I was trying to make. Everyone thinks the world of you, Dean. You're a good man. And believe it or not, everyone knows it – everyone except you, maybe."

A bolt of lightening, followed almost immediately by a crack of thunder, startled them both. It also provided Dean with an easy out from yet another conversation that he didn't want to have, or more precisely, couldn't bring himself to acknowledge.

"Seems like quite a show out there," Dean said, as he got up and walked out to the back patio.

Once outside, he stared off into the distance at the light show. The rain was coming down in sheets now, and the night air had grown so cold that he could see his breath. A shiver ran through him as a brisk wind was being whipped up off the lake. He felt Tony's arms wrap around him, trying to keep him warm.

"I can't remember the last time I felt something as wonderful as you in my arms," Tony said.

Dean turned around and looked into Tony's eyes. "Do you want to know what our biggest problem was? I was with this wonderful man, the man of my dreams really, and whenever you would say something like that, something so perfect and romantic, I just couldn't believe it because you were talking about me."

With that final bit of honesty, he kissed Tony softly on the cheek and walked back inside.

CHAPTER 39

"Lonny was right," Tony said, as he followed Dean back into the house. "You really don't know how extraordinary you are."

"Nah, Lonny had it backwards. I'm actually quite ordinary and he never really understood that."

"I don't fall in love with ordinary people, Dean," Tony said, with a sincerity that took Dean's breath away. Still, he couldn't accept what Tony was saying.

"Well then, Ace, it looks like I fooled you."

"Don't do that. Don't slip into that cavalier, sarcastic tone and jump behind your walls. Talk to me."

"What do you want from me, Tony?" Dean asked, without anger. He really did want to know.

"The truth is, I want you back. I don't think I realized that until tonight, but there it is. I know it may not happen, but I'm being honest. Barring that, I want to know that when we go back to Chicago, you're going to be okay. You seem fine now, but I'm so worried that once you get back home you're going to fall apart again."

"Tony, you could do so much better than me. Why on earth, after everything that has happened, would you want to get back together?"

"Because I love you, that's why."

"It's not magic, Tony. Love doesn't just make everything else go away. It's just a word."

"Why did you break up with me?" Tony asked, taking a turn that Dean wasn't expecting.

"What do you mean?"

"You've already told me that you were looking for a reason to break up with me when you came over that night. My question is why did you want to break up? Were you unhappy? Was it Kurt? Did I come on too strong? What?"

"What does it matter now?"

"Indulge me. And if that isn't a good enough reason, then let's just say you owe me an explanation."

"You won't understand."

"Try me," Tony said. He could tell he was getting to the root of what was going on with Dean and he was desperate to see this through, regardless of the outcome.

Dean stared at Tony and tried to figure out what to say. Finally he decided to just be honest.

"There were two reasons. First, I seem to lose everyone, eventually. My parents, friends to AIDS, Lonny. And every time it happens, I think that it can't possibly hurt as much as all the other times, but of course it does. If I make the decision to end a relationship, at least that is a loss I can control. It's a loss that hurts less than the others. That always worked – until you."

"That's no way to live, Dean. You have to keep trying. It's impossible to just shut down your feelings."

"Well, if I've learned anything lately, I've learned that. But do you understand? Never mind, it's impossible to understand unless you've been there."

"I know that I haven't lost people on the scale that you have, honey. And I can see where eventually you'd have to start thinking that the universe was out to get you, but still there's always hope. I never thought I could feel the kind of love that I felt for Steve again. When he died, I thought, 'well, that's that.' Then you came along and it was like – wow! It was like falling in love for the first time."

"And love is an amazing thing, Tony. It really is. But when it's yanked away from you, again and again and again, it becomes too much to bear. For me, love has always been something that's come with an expiration date."

"But again, if you give up all hope of love, what are you left with? What kind of life does that lead to?"

"Well, obviously, it doesn't do wonders for your mental stability," Dean said, with a slight laugh. "I'm not saying that it makes any sense, Tony, I'm just saying that its how I feel. I just reached a point where love became too much of a risk. Falling in love is great, but losing it was killing me a little bit each time. So add that to the fact that almost everyone looks down on me and you can see where I might not be the most open person in the world."

"What? Where is that coming from?"

"That's the second reason. Do you have any idea what it's like to be average in our circle of friends? To never have quite as much as everyone else? To grow up poor and know that they know that you grew up poor? To rent a small apartment when everyone else owns a nice home? To be single when everyone else is married? To be part of a circle of friends and yet to be different from everyone else? To be less than everyone else?"

"Dean, I can't imagine that anyone thinks of you that way," Tony said, genuinely surprised by how the wonderful man who he loved so dearly perceived himself.

"You can't imagine because you have so much, Tony. You had a husband for the longest time, you're set financially, there is an ease about you that just screams 'I've made it.'"

"Baby, I love you, but I think you're world vision is a bit off-kilter. Do you really think your friends see you that way?"

"Don't get me wrong. I know they love me just as much as

I love them. They probably think I'm cute and funny and fun to be around, recent events not withstanding. But yes, in some ways, I think they look down on me and always have. And they always will until I finally reach a point in my life where I have all the things that they have."

"You know, in Lonnie's letter, he mentioned that you'd been supporting him for a lot of years," Tony said.

"Yeah? So?"

"I'm just thinking you might want to take some of that money that you'd been giving him and give it to a therapist."

For the first time in a long time Dean laughed out loud. It felt good. He knew Tony was probably right, of course, but it didn't alter the reality of how he felt.

"Let's assume for the moment that everything you just said is true," Tony said. "I don't believe it for a second, and I don't think anyone who knows you and loves you feels that way, but let's assume that it is true. I still don't understand why that made you break up with me."

"Because you were too good for me, silly man. I just couldn't imagine what people must have thought when we were together. Like I said before, you could do so much better."

Tony walked over to where Dean was standing and wrapped him in his arms. He kissed him so deeply that it almost hurt. When he finally pulled away, Dean's face was a mixture of happiness and heartache that Tony doubted he would ever understand, but he decided he didn't care.

"Do you know that the only thing I ever thought about you – other than how much I love you – is how proud I was of you. You never talked all that much about your past, but enough that I knew that your life hasn't been so easy. And yet, look what you've done with it. Dean, you have nothing to be ashamed of – nothing. You are a good man. I know it sounds simple, but it's the best compliment I can think to give anyone. You are a good man. I wish you could see you the way I do. You'd be amazed."

Dean's teary eyes had finally started to spill over, but for the first time in as long as he could remember, they weren't tears of sadness. Maybe it was time to stop focusing so much on what he'd lost and start focusing on what he'd found.

"I do love you, Tony," he said, simply.

"I know, baby," Tony said, with a smile.

They kissed again and didn't stop until many hours later.

* * * * *

The last thing in the world that Dean wanted to do the following morning was wake up. The storm had passed and the sun was shining, but still Dean refused to open his eyes. The wonderful sensation of his head on Tony's chest, which he had missed so much, was too enjoyable to let go of so easily. But there was in incessant tapping sound that was driving him crazy. He grudgingly opened his eyes and sat up. Looking to his left, he saw Moose, Peter and Terrell peering at him through the bedroom window, smiling and waving.

"Oh for the love of God," Dean muttered as he flopped back onto the bed.

"What?" Tony mumbled, as he snuggled back up to Dean.

"We have company."

Tony bolted upright and grabbed the sheet before their friends got an eyeful of 'morning Tony.'

Dean and Tony waved their friends off and told them to go to the front door. Hastily pulling on robes, they made their way to the living room and let the rowdy crew in. Their intimate morning had become an impromptu brunch for eight.

"Blame me," Moose said to Dean, as soon as he made it through the door. "I was worried sick about you. I woke everyone up and we hit the road – "

"At five a.m.," Erik grumbled.

" – and drove straight up."

Moose grabbed Dean and hugged him fiercely.

"We'd ask how you're doing, Dean," Peter said, with a

smile towards Tony, "But it looks like you're doing better."

"I'm fine, thanks. I really am sorry for everything that happened the last few days," Dean said.

"Don't worry about it," Kurt said, as he gave Dean a kiss on the cheek. "Considering everything that you've been going through, it's understandable. Are we good?"

"Yeah, we're good," Dean said.

"I'm not good, I'm fucking starving," Bill said.

The group made their way into the kitchen and began cooking and talking over each other and laughing. It was a moment of pure happiness for Dean, and he embraced it. He loved them all. Tony came up behind him. They stood and watched their friends for a few minutes. For just a moment, thoughts of Lonny passed through Dean's mind. But instead of bringing sadness, a smile came to his lips. He wasn't alone, he realized, and that made all the difference in the world.